HEART AT RISK

BY
HELEN SHELTON

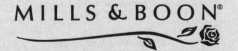

MILLS & BOON®

First published in Great Britain 2000
Harlequin Mills & Boon Limited,
Eton House, 18-24 Paradise Road, Richmond, Surrey TW9 1SR

© Poppytech Services Pty, Ltd 2000

ISBN 0 263 82248 6

Set in Times Roman 10½ on 12 pt.
03-0007-53943

Printed and bound in Spain
by Litografia Rosés, S.A., Barcelona

CHAPTER ONE

IN THE pale light filtering through the grimed and narrow window above the cubicle's chipped basin Annabel looked fragile and timid. Her hair shimmered like a copper halo around her head but the shadows under her cheek-bones had turned into great caverns and her pale-fringed grey eyes looked like huge, frightened pools in a stark white face.

Disgusted with her pathetic appearance, she rubbed the heels of her hands roughly across her cheeks to draw some colour then tried narrowing her eyes a little. Since that wasn't that much better she lifted a hand back to her face and cupped her chin and the side of her cheek, supporting her elbow with her opposite hand. If she couldn't manage robust and confident she could at least strive for intellectual rather than waif-like.

'Hello, Luke. *Hello!* Hello!' She grimaced. She sounded like a chicken with a sore throat. She took a step back then tried that again with a lower pitch and a more formal address. 'Hello, Professor. Welcome to St Peter's.' She lowered her arm slowly and put her hand out to shake it, then withdrew it jerkily and returned to her previous position. 'Me?' She lifted one of her shoulders. 'Oh, I'm fine,' she murmured. 'Yes, fine. Just fine. Yes, only six years. Can you believe it? It seems like an infinity ago.'

The sound of the outer door to the restroom swinging open sent her spinning away from the basin, and by the time the inner door was shoved wide she was wiping her dry hands on a paper towel, a fixed smile in place.

'Oh, hi, Dr Stuart!' Hannah, her registrar, came rushing

in, her colour high. 'You're late for the reception. Are there problems on the wards?'

'None I've been told about,' Annabel said unsteadily. She held the door open. 'I'm on my way to meet Professor Geddes now.' She noted the flushed animation illuminating the younger doctor's normally placid face. 'I take it he hasn't left yet.'

'Oh, no, he's still there,' Hannah told her breathlessly. 'Mmm.'

Annabel studied her briefly, then turned away. 'I'd best get along then.'

The seminar room where the welcoming reception was being held was twenty yards off the main hospital corridor in the direction of the administrative offices and Annabel could hear the buzz of excited conversation from outside the closed doors. Taking a deep breath, she opened the door, accepted the unwanted polystyrene cup of orange juice someone shoved into her hand, looked quickly around the gathered crowd, then managed a tense smile for the elderly consultant who immediately started making his way through the throng towards her.

'Annabel!' Harry exclaimed. 'Where've you been hiding? You must be the only doctor in the place who hasn't rushed up to be introduced to your new boss yet.'

Tempted, for what felt like the hundredth time, to flee, Annabel started to mutter some brief excuse, only Harry's hand curved around to the small of her back and he propelled her firmly forward when what she really wanted was to make her own way in her own time. Like perhaps in another six years. Or maybe in twelve. Or, better, given the goose-bumps already breaking out all the way from her arms to her ankles as she felt Luke's attention swing to her, in a couple of decades or more.

She'd assumed that time would have granted her some

'Annie.'

Luke's shrewdly observant eyes narrowed fractionally. 'It's been a long time. You look...very different. I barely recognised you. How have you been?'

'Fine. I'm very well, in fact,' Annie added. 'I think better than I've ever been at any time in my life before.'

He tilted his head. 'Really?'

'Really,' she confirmed stiffly. 'You seem to find that surprising, Luke. Are you disappointed? Did you expect to find me dressed in black and still in mourning for you?'

'*Still* in mourning for me?' He stared her down. 'That's an odd thing to say, Annie. Are you trying to tell me you did once mourn?'

A New Zealand doctor with restless feet, **Helen Shelton** has lived and worked in Britain and travelled widely. Married to an Australian she met while on safari in Africa, she recently moved to Sydney, where they plan to settle for a little while at least. She has always been an enthusiastic reader and writer, and inspiration for the background for her Medical Romances™ comes directly from her own experiences working in hospitals in several countries around the world.

Recent titles by the same author:

COURTING CATHIE*
IDYLLIC INTERLUDE
A TIMELY AFFAIR
A SURGEON FOR SUSAN

*Bachelor Doctors

degree of immunity to him, but her hope that the years
might have thickened his middle or thinned his hair had
been forlorn. His hair, although shorter than he used to
wear it, was still thick and dark and the superb fit of the
expensive-looking, moss-coloured suit he wore told her
that, however hard he'd worked during his years in Boston,
he'd still found time for his squash.

Not, though, that she'd needed to see him herself to
know he hadn't exactly grown ordinary. The frenetic excitement of at least half the hospital's staff these past four
days had served as an unpleasant reminder of Luke's effect
on women.

Good looks and an athletic body combined with intelli-
gence and power, was always attractive in a man, she conceded. But Luke's appeal was heightened by his cold in-
difference to his own attractions and the fascination they
provoked. His priority in his life was his career, and women
who were challenged by that and brave enough to go after
him regardless invariably ended up with singed wings and
emotions in tatters.

And Annabel knew how it felt to be driven to pursue
Luke. Remembering how brazenly she'd once chased him,
it could make her skin burn.

'You're just about the only female member of staff who
hasn't been trying to bribe me to let her jump the queue to
meet him.' Harry, murmuring close to her ear, sounded
proud and she realised he was taking personal credit for
Luke's popularity. 'Even the clerical staff have been falling
over themselves.'

Annabel sent him a quick, dry look. Poor Harry, she
thought weakly. Did he think the secretarial staff were
flocking to admire Luke's distinguished *academic* achievements?

With all the time she'd spent lately practising neutral

greetings and looking composed in front of mirrors she'd
thought she had a good chance of handling this first meeting without actually making an idiot of herself, but when
she lifted guarded grey eyes and met Luke's enigmatic
green regard head on for the first time, the impact of him,
the total, disconcerting *familiarity* of him, slammed into her
brain like a lorry into a twig.

She faltered, momentarily broadsided, but thankfully
Harry seemed not to notice. 'Annabel Stuart, this is Luke
Geddes,' he pronounced, although, of course, there'd never
been any doubt about the identity of the man waiting silently beside him. '*Professor* Luke Geddes, that is,' Harry
added with a beam, pushing his spectacles a little higher
on his rounded nose and stressing the title with such characteristic pomposity that Annabel, despite her numbness,
was aware of a surge of fondness for the elderly physician.

'Naturally we're thrilled to have him now on staff,'
Harry burbled on. 'Luke, you'll remember I've mentioned
Annabel to you already. She might be young but she's one
of our finest cardiologists. Of course, since your spheres of
clinical work are similar, the two of you will be working
closely together from now on. I'm sure Annabel's keen to
show you around the place, Luke. She'll be eager to help
you settle in.'

I'd rather eat worms, Annabel thought numbly, but she
confined her greeting to a strictly conventional, practised,
if husky, 'Hello, Professor Geddes. Hello. Welcome to St
Peter's.'

Determined to avoid alerting her colleagues to their previous relationship, she'd decided in advance to use Luke's
formal title. Although Harry had murmured an apology and
turned away to talk to one of the senior surgeons, meaning
he probably couldn't hear her, her brain wasn't working
well enough yet to allow any deviation from her plan.

Shifting her orange juice into her left hand, she extended her right. The last thing she wanted was physical contact with Luke, but they were surrounded by people and she was determined to be seen to be doing the right thing.

'Annie.' Luke's shrewdly observant eyes narrowed fractionally but he shook the hand she'd offered him without hesitation. His grip was steady and dry and firm enough for her to be overwhelmingly aware of his strength, without him actually crushing her hand. Proof that her own palm was heated and damp, her grip too weakly tentative to be pleasant, came with the swift way he released her again.

'It's been a long time,' he added, the attractive deepness of his voice emphasising the strengthening of the American accent he'd always possessed, even when he'd lived in Britain, courtesy of his Minnesota childhood and American mother. 'You look…very different. I barely recognised you.' His regard where it dropped to assess her fell far short of approving and she felt herself beginning to bristle the way only Luke could make her bristle. 'How have you been?'

She sent another nervous look towards Harry, reassuring herself, since Luke clearly didn't share her determination to keep their knowledge of each other private, that he was still otherwise occupied, before responding tightly, 'Fine.' She knew, and his critical inspection reminded her again, that she had changed these past years. However, unlike Luke, she considered her carefully groomed short hairstyle and her respectable-length beige dress a vast improvement on the tousled tresses and provocative outfits she'd favoured when she'd been young and confident enough to carry them off.

'I'm very well, in fact,' she added unevenly. 'I think better than I've ever been at any time in my life before.'

He tilted his head, his green eyes narrowing again. 'Really?'

'Really,' she confirmed stiffly. 'You seem to find that surprising, Luke. Are you disappointed? Did you expect to find me dressed in black and still in mourning for you?'

'*Still* in mourning for me?' He stared her down. 'That's an odd thing to say, Annie. Are you trying to tell me you did once mourn?'

'*Annie?*' Harry turned back to them unexpectedly and to her despair he'd caught Luke's disturbing shortening of her name. 'Have you and Annabel met already, Luke? Sorry. I didn't realise.'

Luke met Annabel's panicked look with a bland smile. 'Annabel and I go way back,' he said smoothly.

'You didn't mention that, Annabel.' Harry, she saw, when she tore her eyes away from Luke's dry regard, looked astonished. 'I'm sure you've never said—'

'We haven't seen each other in years,' Annabel interrupted, desperate to divert him before Luke told him any more. 'Luke and I both trained at the Free,' she added, referring to another London teaching hospital in what she hoped was a suitably offhand way. 'Of course he was a few years ahead of me—'

'More than a few,' Luke contributed pleasantly. 'Annabel and I met when I was a senior medical registrar at the Free and I lectured her class, Harry. She was a final-year medical student at the time.'

Harry's normally benign expression had turned from surprise to frank accusation. 'But you've never said anything, Annabel. Even when you knew I was flying to Boston to interview Luke you didn't tell me you were friends.'

Friends? Annabel strove for what she hoped looked like a dismissive smile. 'We *used* to know each other, Harry.

We don't know each other now. It's six years since Luke and I last met. I didn't realise it was necessary to say anything.'

She knew that Harry, despite the fact that as of this week he was passing the reins of his command on to Luke and taking partial retirement, liked to think he was up with all the happenings at the hospital and with her. In his self-proclaimed position as benevolent mentor to her career, he took a keen interest in her and her life and she was sorry if her reticence about Luke had offended him.

The truth was, she'd had enough to cope with just coming to terms with Luke's appointment, without the added burden of trying to work out how best to explain their past relationship to the rest of the staff. Explain it, that was, in a way that wouldn't set them both up for months of unpleasant gossip.

She loved working at St Peter's. It was one of the finest specialist heart hospitals in the world and she felt wonderfully at home here. But in small hospitals, and in this small hospital in particular, practically everyone on staff knew everyone else. It wasn't easy to keep secrets. Especially one as juicy as this one.

'It really was a long, long time ago,' she added quietly, directing another pointed look towards Luke. 'I was surprised when I heard you were returning to London, Luke. I assumed you'd decided to make your career permanently in the US.'

'I've been considering coming back to London for a year.' He glanced at Harry. 'I've been away too long. I made enquiries when this job was advertised and Harry made me a good offer.'

'Especially tempting since it meant coming back to one of the best hospitals in the country,' Harry said heartily, apparently recovered from his shock over Luke's announcement. 'We might not be enormous but we're perfectly formed. Just like me.' He tapped the top of his bald, rounded head and chuckled at his own joke.

'We're absolutely delighted to have snared you, Luke. I know for a fact we weren't the only ones making offers and we're very glad you chose us. It's an honour, passing my job on to a clinician of your reputation. Now, Annabel…' Harry waggled his brows at her above his spectacles. 'I think Luke's met everyone. You were the last to arrive by a long way.' He glanced around the other groups of doctors at the welcoming reception, as if making sure of that.

'Why don't you take him around the place a bit? Show him the labs and clinic rooms and the things he really needs to see. I've given him a quick general tour of the hospital but, since you're friends, you'll be able to give him a more personal, insider's slant on everything.'

Annabel felt a pang of something behind her breastbone like indigestion. She took a hasty sip of her neglected juice, attempting to buy time while she considered how best to dodge Harry's suggestion, but the drink had turned unpleasantly warm while she'd been holding it and she put the cup down onto the table beside her. The liquid, given the current nervous state of her stomach, would only add to her nausea. 'I expect tomorrow would be a more suitable time,' she began determinedly.

Luke interrupted with a deceptively benign, 'Now suits me.' Imitating her own movement with her juice, he put down the cup of what looked like beer which he'd been holding on the table beside hers. 'Unless, Annie, you're in a hurry to get home. To a husband perhaps? Do you have children now?'

Annabel met his regard warily, wondering if his question was simply the polite, concerned enquiry he'd made it seem, or if he could actually be curious about her life now.

But that, of course, was ridiculous. Why would he care? Self-consciously aware that both men were waiting for her to continue, and that she'd allowed the silence to stretch fractionally too far, she said simply, 'I'm not married and no one's expecting me home. Naturally, if now suits you I'm happy to show you around.' That at least would get them away from witnesses. 'Harry, we won't be long. Will you still be here or...?'

'I think I'll just drink up and be on my way,' the older doctor said sagely. 'I'm not as young as I used to be. I need my sleep these days. I'll see you in the morning, Annabel. And you, Luke. Goodnight.'

Annabel, tensely conscious of every one of Luke's easy strides beside her, waited until they were a little way along the corridor connecting the administrative part of the hospital—where the reception had been held—with the ward and clinical blocks.

'Of course, we both know there's no need for me to show you much of the place,' she said stiltedly, sliding a quick sideways look up to meet his neutral perusal. 'You did work here for a year as a registrar after all. Not a lot's changed around here since then.'

'How long have you been here?'

'Coming up for eighteen months as a consultant.' She'd spent most of her registrar years rotating between hospitals affiliated to the Royal Free Hospital in Hampstead but had accepted a specialist cardiology job at St Peter's in the final year of her training. 'I came here towards the end of my specialist training and applied for this job when one of the consultants retired. Naturally, we're a high-tech unit, but you'll still find this a pleasantly relaxed, friendly place to work. I'm sure you'll enjoy your time here.'

For however long he lasted, she added mentally. While even being in a position to be considered for the position

of Medical Director at St Peter's would have been for most
of them the absolute pinnacle of their careers, she knew
Luke well enough to know he'd merely view the position
as a stepping stone. He was powerfully ambitious and there
were bigger hospitals in the world and cardiac units with
higher profiles. She didn't expect him to stay long.

'These are all part of the rehabilitation unit,' she commented, indicating the two wards branching off as the corridor entered the ward block proper. 'I'm sure you'll remember the layout of the place once you've had a chance
to refresh your memory although when you were here this
area was probably smaller. There's a counselling team
down in here which is tied in with the unit as well, plus
social services, and we have a supervising psychiatrist,
along with a good team of nurse therapists.

'We take rehab very seriously these days, of course. The
staff are dedicated and enthusiastic and accept referrals for
everyone from our babies and their families up through the
transplant cases, with donors and patients and families, as
well as the usual sort of work with heart attack rehabilitation. It's a big unit. Since you were here last it's been
extended out into the new building through there. You'll
find it interesting to have a look around. We run night
classes and weekend workshops for ex-patients and new
referrals. We have—'

'You don't have to sell me on the place, Annabel. I
agreed to take the job three months ago.'

Annabel felt herself flush. He'd stopped, meaning she
felt she had to stop, too, but she kept her eyes focused on
the tight knot in his silver and green diamond-patterned tie.
'I'm simply trying to do as Harry asked—'

'There's no need to go to this extreme.'

'Harry asked me to show you around,' she protested unevenly. 'As I was about to say, I'm only trying to do what I was asked—'

'Why are you so angry?'

'I'm not.' She drew in a long breath, then lifted her eyes, braving his green inspection with what felt like rapidly dwindling courage. 'Or at least not the way you think,' she said stiltedly. 'But…I thought the least you would do is make sure the first time we met again was somewhere private.' The words came surging out of her in a rush.

'That was difficult for me, Luke. Very difficult. I was sick with nerves. The last thing in the world I wanted was to have to come up to you in a room full of other people and pretend to be full of jolly *bonhomie*. I'm sure you're very busy at present but still I'd have appreciated a little more consideration—'

'I didn't know about that reception,' he interrupted. 'The first I heard of it was when Harry sprang it on me this afternoon. I've only been in the country since Friday morning—'

'And now it's Monday evening!' she emphasised. 'And you've been in and out of the hospital dozens of times. Almost everyone's seen you—they've all been talking. I was here on Friday and I was home all weekend. I waited there deliberately, expecting you to call.'

'You could have found out where I was.'

'I'm not the one suddenly arriving out of the blue after six years,' she reminded him, her tone sharpening.

'I've already explained about the reception.' When her face stayed stony, he sighed. 'Annie, stop it. There's no need for this and I don't want to argue with you. This is awkward for me, too.'

'I doubt it.'

He gave a short, impatient sigh. 'I'm sorry tonight was hard for you but you're making it more difficult by playing

childish games about how well you know me and by trying
to provoke an argument—'

'By the way I prefer Annabel these days.' The sound of
Luke's attractively deep voice using the abbreviated version
roused unwelcome, disturbingly intimate memories, unsettling
her when she most wanted to stay chillingly professional.
'Please.'

His mouth tightened fractionally but he let her plea pass
without comment. 'I didn't even know you'd specialised in
cardiology until Harry mentioned your name to me unexpectedly
three months ago. As soon as I discovered you
were on staff here I wrote immediately. Since you couldn't
bring yourself to pen even a postcard reply, don't lose it
because I've turned up. You had the opportunity to say you
couldn't handle me here—'

'Oh, yes, and that would have made me hugely popular,'
she responded. In his painfully formal letter he'd written
that if she really felt they wouldn't be able to work together
he would respect that and withdraw from the job. 'I had no
choice,' she protested. 'You sent that letter after you'd
signed your employment contract.'

'Contracts can be broken,' he countered irritably. 'Naturally,
I would have had to explain you felt it would be
impossible—'

'Turning me into a laughing stock,' she interjected. 'My
life here would be unbearable if I did something like that.
Getting you here is an enormous coup for St Peter's, Luke.
They'll be crowing for years about it. The great Luke
Geddes, Director of Clinical Cardiology and Professor of
Medicine at Harvard University. You might think of yourself
as an American but you trained here so you're still
considered the local boy made good and a role model for
us all to aspire to.

'Most of the physicians here are still reeling with shock

you didn't pick up the Nobel medicine prize last year. Your name is whispered in hallowed voices around these parts. If it came down to a choice between losing you or me there wouldn't be a soul in the trust stupid enough to argue my feeble merits.'

'You're a gifted cardiologist—'

'Don't patronise me,' she snapped.

'I meant it,' he retorted, equally harshly. 'You've done well for yourself and you're still young. You've years ahead of you yet. From what I've heard since I've arrived, for a junior consultant you have an excellent reputation—'

'I'm a competent, diligent physician,' she interrupted, lowering her voice abruptly as a porter rounded the corner of the corridor ahead of them, bearing a broad, steel meals trolley. 'I'm a competent physician,' she repeated, striving for a more reasonable tone of voice lest they be overheard. 'Nothing more. But since we can't all be gifted geniuses, I've learned to live with my limitations. Now, can we just get on with the tour, please?'

His eyes had flashed at her bitter reference to him, terms she'd flung at him more than once in the past, but this time, for once, he let it pass.

They moved back against opposite walls of the corridor to allow the porter to pass freely, and when the trolley had moved away Luke was studying her speculatively, his regard sombre, his mood clearly now more subdued. 'It doesn't have to be like this, Annie. *Annabel*,' he added impatiently when her regard sharpened.

'And it won't be. It won't be like this.' Annabel dropped her head, letting out her breath in a long, weary sigh, mortified now as his words brought home to her the unpleasant truth that as usual she'd allowed her reaction to him to goad her into losing control.

She hadn't meant that to happen. She hadn't even imagined it could have. She'd been determined not to allow the past to spill over into the present, not when they now had to work together. For the sake of her own emotional health she meant to avoid him wherever possible, and when she couldn't she meant to keep relations carefully impersonal.

'I'm sorry,' she added dully. 'Tonight has gone... horribly wrong. I shouldn't have snapped at you. I meant to be...' she lifted her hands in a helpless sort of gesture, unsure how best to convey to him her apology was sincere '...controlled. I'm afraid it seems as if it's going to take a little bit of time for me to get used to you actually being around again. But, rest assured, I will do my best not to allow our past relationship to affect our work.'

The narrowing of his eyes suggested her little speech had surprised him. 'Where do you live now?'

She blinked, bemused by that. 'What?'

'I'll take you home.'

'No, thank you.' These last few minutes had proved how brittle her control was tonight and she certainly wasn't about to encourage more discussion. 'I have my own car. Besides, there's nothing to talk about—'

'A bar, a café if it has to be. Or I'm staying at a hotel until I have a chance to look for somewhere—'

'No!' She felt colour rushing into her face at the speculative look her outburst provoked. 'No,' she repeated, more reasonably this time. 'I've given this a great deal of thought since I heard about your appointment and I'm convinced it's a bad idea to make any attempt to rehash old memories. The past is the past. I think we should begin completely afresh with a new, purely professional relationship. As far as I'm aware, no one here knows about us so we can simply act as if we've never met before.'

'No one knows?' He seemed surprised. 'I realised pretty

quickly poor old Harry hasn't a clue, but you mean you haven't told *anyone*?'

'It's never seemed relevant to mention it.' When she'd changed hospitals to work at St Peter's it had been like starting afresh for her. She'd largely cut herself off from people they'd mixed with when she and Luke had been together. Not that that had been such a hardship since most of them had been Luke's friends really, rather than hers. 'I'm sure there're people still working at the Free who remember,' she reflected, 'but, as far as I know, no one here knows.'

'And you're expecting me to keep it a secret now?'

'Not a secret.' She didn't want him to lie to anyone, but surely asking him not to volunteer the information wasn't such an imposition? 'But I don't see that one failed little marriage years ago is anyone's business but ours. You know what this place is like. People are friendly but they also talk. It'll cause unpleasant gossip—'

'A nine-minute wonder.' Luke made an impatient noise. 'So what? You're nuts, Annabel.' He sounded very American. 'You're acting as though it's a big deal and it isn't. Couples divorce all the time. Doctors especially. Nobody's going to judge either of us. Pretending it never happened is only making it look more significant than it was.'

'And, of course, you don't consider it at all significant in your life,' she said tightly. 'To you I was simply an inconvenience—'

'I didn't say that.' Six years ago he would have flared, as she just had, at that, and they would have rowed, inevitably they'd have rowed, but now his tone remained entirely reasonable. 'Don't put words into my mouth. I never liked it before and I don't like it now.'

'Then perhaps you'll understand how I feel when I say

I don't like being gossiped about,' she countered dully, lowering her head and jerking her rebellious thoughts away from the intrusive recall of the powerful way they'd invariably made up after their fights. Until the last one, of course, when there'd been no making up. He hadn't even been in the country for the divorce. His recent letter, confirming his new appointment and containing nothing in the way of personal greetings or good wishes, had been the first communication between them in years.

Not that that meant she hadn't known where he'd been or what he'd been doing. Given that she'd gone on to train in the same field, and he and his team at Harvard were among the dominant influences in the modern practice of heart medicine, she couldn't have helped following his career.

'I dislike the thought of people knowing and discussing personal things about me,' she added reasonably. 'Please, try just for once seeing things from my point of view. If someone asks you outright, fine. I know you won't lie and I'm not asking you to. All I'm asking is that you don't volunteer our history unasked.'

'Fine.' He spoke wearily. 'If that's the sort of thing that pushes your happy buttons these days, so be it. Anything for an easy life. Can we get on with the tour now, please?'

'But before when I said just that—' Calculating from his narrowed eyes that to continue would have been unwise, she broke off before she reminded him that it was he who'd interrupted her tour earlier and he who'd sustained their confrontation when she'd tried to make him turn from it.

Turning her back on him, she walked off down the corridor again. 'Paediatrics down there,' she informed him, determined to do the job properly regardless of what, if any, attention he paid to her spiel. 'Two full wards as well as a twelve-bed specialist children's surgical unit and paediatric intensive care. Kids having major surgery still have two dedicated acute beds in the cardiothoracic intensive care unit, then they're transferred here when they're stable.

'You'll find the nurses are very switched on down here. They're the best I've ever worked with. There's an eight-bed neonatal unit for our babies and off there to the right are the rest of the administration offices, as well as a few suites for out-of-town parents and anyone staying over.'

She felt him following her through into the main five-storied ward block. 'Outpatients, exercise and ECG rooms and X-Ray, where you'll find three catheter labs.' The cardiac cath. suite was basically a theatre unit used for sterile procedures within the X-Ray department. 'You'll find basically everything you'll need for outpatients down here.'

Built in a cross-like shape, each floor of St Peter's had four wards or departments branched off the central core, which contained waiting areas and the lifts and stairwells. Not happy with the idea of being stuck with Luke in a confined space, she veered away from the bank of lifts and made for the heavy door that opened onto the stairwell.

'Medical and Surgical Intensive Cares,' she recited carefully as they rounded the landing on the first floor. 'Largely just for ventilated patients, although when we're busy we tend to stretch that. Coronary Care's here, too, plus the transplant unit, although to get to that you have to go via the airlock doors around the other side. The transplant ward itself and all cardiac surgery wards, plus Pathology and all the labs,' she said briskly, as they reached the second floor.

'Four medical wards,' she explained at the next floor. 'J, K, M and P. You'll probably end up, like me, with most of your inpatients on either J or M. You'll find your way around them quickly enough even if you can't remember them now. Most of the offices are here, too, along the north wing, but I assume you'll be taking over Harry's big one which is up on the top floor.

'Private medicine and day surgery,' she continued, opening the door on the top floor for them because it seemed preferable to spending more time in the narrow stairwell. 'That's it really, I think, apart from a couple of buildings scattered around the grounds here and there, including the library, post-graduate centre and the student teaching rooms. Mostly, though, we tend to use the ward seminar rooms for small-group teaching. The staff canteen's down near Rehab but there's a shop and public café in the reception area near Outpatients which both do better food than the hospital stuff.

'Well, that's it, then.' She wiped her hands together carefully. Luke hadn't spoken since their confrontation in the corridor and his expression now wasn't encouraging, but he was here to stay now for however long he chose to remain at St Peter's and she'd go mad if she let herself keep worrying about what he was thinking. 'I expect you'll find it easier to see the place in more detail when you're actually working. Feel free to ask anybody anything. You might think you don't know many of us yet, but all of us know who you are.'

'Where are you going now?'

'Home.' She cut him off before he could repeat his earlier suggestion that they meet outside the hospital then checked her watch with deliberate thoroughness. 'In fact, I'm in rather a hurry. I have an early start in the morning so unless you've any questions about the hospital...?' When he said nothing she added quietly, 'I do appreciate you making the effort to call me Annabel, Luke. I realise it's another syllable you'll have to add into your busy life but if you say it quite fast it's not so much effort and it means a lot to me.'

'You can go now.' He opened the door they'd just come
through for her. 'I get the message, *Annie*. Loud and clear.'

Annabel opened her mouth to voice some protest about
his use of 'Annie' again, but the silent warning in his eyes
made her decide to close her lips again and, with careful
dignity, she fled.

CHAPTER TWO

'WHAT did you think of him?' Geoffrey asked, cornering her the next morning in her office before her ward round.

Annabel stiffened. 'Who?'

'Oh, come on.' Her colleague's eyes blinked owlishly at her behind his round horn-rimmed spectacles. 'The big American. The brilliant Professor. Dr Superman. Didn't you go to the reception yesterday? What do you think? How is he?'

'What did *you* think?' Annabel asked guardedly.

'I haven't met him yet.' Geoffrey rolled his eyes as if he found it incredible—although she couldn't imagine why—that she hadn't realised that. 'I've been away for six days. You've been covering my patients. Earth to Annabel. Earth to Annabel. Are you with me yet?'

'Sorry.' She felt herself flush. 'I forgot.' Geoffrey had been at a conference in Bristol and had eschewed the commute in favour of staying at the conference hotel until late the night before. She shook her head a little, hoping that might help clear it. 'He seems fine,' she said slowly.

Geoffrey rolled his eyes again. 'Fine,' he echoed cheerfully. 'She thinks he's fine. Come on, Annabel, you must be able to do better than that. You're the third person I've asked this morning. The first one said she was still swooning from passing him in the corridor on Friday morning and the second one's contemplating divorcing her husband and three children so she can make a play for him with a clear conscience.

'Now, much as I appreciate you trying to protect my

24

fragile ego, you can tell me what you really think, you know. I won't challenge the man to a duel or anything like that. At least, not unless he tries to sweep you off your feet.'

Annabel choked. For a few seconds they were both distracted, she with coughing and then getting her breath again and Geoffrey with finding her some water to swallow. 'The one thing in this world,' she pronounced hoarsely, after swallowing a generous mouthful of the drink he rushed her from the cooler outside the office, 'that I can promise you without hesitation is that the only place Luke Geddes will ever contemplate sweeping me is out of his way.'

'Phew!' Grinning, Geoffrey made a mock forehead-wiping gesture. 'That's a relief. You didn't think much of him, then?'

'He's an attractive man,' she conceded cautiously, since to deny that would obviously be suspicious.

'But not your type?'

'*Definitely* not my type,' she avowed. She doubted she'd ever be completely over Luke but there'd been a time when she'd loved him so blindly her passion had rendered her oblivious to the irreparable flaws in their relationship. Romantic emotions and sex couldn't sustain a marriage when a couple had such different expectations and were as fundamentally incompatible as she and Luke had been. If she'd only realised that sooner she could have saved him considerable inconvenience and herself a great deal of anguish.

Geoffrey, on the other hand, was—*nothing*—nothing, like her ex-husband. Which was probably why she liked him so much. Geoffrey was mild and undemanding, supportive, kind and sweet and entirely lacking Luke's particularly ruthless brand of driving ambition. Geoffrey was a wonderful colleague and, more than that, he was a friend, and since she didn't have many of those these days she treasured him doubly.

On an impulse she reached up and touched his smooth cheek. 'You're a very nice man,' she said softly.

'Marry me, then,' he came back swiftly.

She recoiled. 'Geoffrey—'

'Sex would do in the meantime while you think about it.'

Her eyes went so wide they hurt. She took another hasty step back. 'Geoffrey, I really would prefer you didn't say those sorts—'

'I know. I know.' Backing away, he held up his palms defensively although he'd started laughing. 'Relax, Annabel. You know I'm only teasing. But if you ever decide to unlock that metaphorical chastity belt of yours...'

'You could do much better than me, you know.' Flushing hotly, Annabel collected the last of the notes she needed and followed him to the door. 'Why don't you try Miriam Frost?' she asked, referring to the charge nurse on one of the paediatric wards as she pulled her office door shut behind her. 'She still seems interested in you. She's very pretty.'

'I like Miriam but she doesn't have big grey pools of eyes and a body to die for,' he pronounced mournfully.

Annabel froze. 'Have you been drinking?'

'Pepsi.' He grinned. 'It was all that was left in the machine and I had a couple of cans. I'm high on sugar and caffeine.'

'I think you might be extremely high.'

'Which doesn't mean you don't have a figure to die for.'

She stared at him, bewildered. 'Geoffrey, you don't know anything about my body. You've never even seen me in a swimming costume.'

'I'm a man, aren't I? I've got X-ray eyes.' Still grinning,

he scanned her figure with cheeky assessment. 'Behind those long dresses and that big white coat there's a taut, silky young body, begging to be let loose.'

Annabel rolled her eyes. 'With an imagination like that you should be in cosmetic surgery, not cardiology. I'll see you in clinic.' After their respective ward rounds they were both due in Outpatients for the rest of the morning. 'Are you going to make it to the Dean's lecture?'

'Wouldn't miss it for the world.' He waved as he strode away, his grin telling her he hadn't forgotten it was her turn do deliver the weekly lunch-hour lecture session that day.

Her registrar and senior house officer were waiting on the ward. Part of being a specialist heart hospital was that all junior medical staff had to have obtained their full medical registration. Because that meant they couldn't appoint junior house officers, routine ward work was generally the domain of the senior house officers, qualified doctors who'd already done one or more years of post-graduate training.

The hospital functioned as a tertiary referral centre—meaning they took referrals from other hospitals rather than through self-presentations or the ambulance services—so they had no walk-in emergency department. Apart from direct referrals from other hospitals—from London as well as the rest of the UK and frequently abroad—the only other routes for admissions were through GPs when the patients were known to them already or via the outpatient clinics held by the various consultants attached to St Peter's.

Her senior house officer had just finished reviewing a woman Annabel had admitted directly from her clinic the afternoon before. 'Daisy's improved a lot overnight, Dr Stuart.'

Annabel nodded. Daisy Miller was a twenty-year-old woman with heart failure secondary to a dilated cardiomyopathy, essentially a condition where the heart became so enlarged and stretched it couldn't function properly.

Hundreds of possible causes for Daisy's illness were known, including exposure to myriad toxins and viruses and other infections and even immune reactions to insect bites. But with Daisy, just as in more than three-quarters of Annabel's other young patients with the same condition, none of the tests she and her predecessor at St Peter's had performed had given them any information about what the specific cause had been in her case.

Daisy had been waiting now almost two years for a heart transplant. When Annabel had seen her urgently the day before she'd been severely breathless from a build-up of fluid on her lungs and around her body.

'Her chest X-ray this morning's definitely clearer.' The younger doctor held two films up to the back-lit X-ray screen so Annabel could assess them and compare the changes. 'She wants to ask you if she can please leave the ward to go out with a special friend to a movie tonight.'

'A *special* friend?' Annabel, agreeing with the other doctor's assessment of the X-ray, looked away from it, her brows lifting. Friends, with Daisy, invariably meant men friends. 'What's happened to poor Jason?'

Hannah, her registrar, pulled a face. She drew a dramatic finger across her throat. 'Ditched,' she pronounced. '"Too clingy", Daisy decided. There's been one in between, but if you ask me this latest one's the best yet. He's a football player. A real, professional one. And it seems serious. Daisy met him at that fund-raising telethon a couple of months ago. I saw him last night and I can understand the attraction. He's got a body you would not believe.'

Annabel smiled. 'Trust Daisy,' she said lightly. Despite struggling with a heart condition that would have kept most people housebound, Daisy, a gorgeous and lively young woman, threw every tiny ounce of energy she could muster into maintaining her busy social life and fund-raising for one of the charities supporting research into heart disease. 'Well, considering she was too breathless to talk yesterday, let alone walk, if she's well enough this morning to be wanting to go out to movies we've done some good. Let's go and see her.'

Daisy did look better. The day before her skin had been grey and bloated but this morning some of her colour was back and most of her swelling had resolved.

'And it's very important, Dr Stuart.' Daisy sent her a beseeching look when Annabel lifted her head from examining her neck and heart and listening to the back of her chest. 'I've been looking forward to it for ages. It's a première. There'll be movie stars there and everything. And it's only in Leicester Square. If I get sick or anything it'll only take me fifteen minutes or so to get back here in a cab.'

'I don't see that it'll do any harm,' said Annabel slowly. Daisy had improved overnight, and even if that improvement was, as they all knew, temporary, a few hours away would be a good test before she considered discharging her again. She smiled at her patient's delighted shriek. 'Promise me you won't do anything silly, or is that asking too much?'

'Silly?' Daisy, still grinning, rolled her eyes dramatically. 'It's only a movie.'

Annabel sent her juniors a dry look. 'Apparently your date has a body I would not believe.'

Daisy flicked her blonde curls back behind her shoulders with a giggle. 'I promise not to exhaust myself,' she vowed. 'I'll be back by midnight.'

'Make it eleven.' Annabel flicked through the folder containing the ward's drug charts until she came to Daisy's prescription chart. She crossed off the intravenous diuretic she'd added to the regime the day before and replaced it with the oral version. 'I'll have a chat with Mr Grant and let him know you're here.' Tony Grant was the transplant surgeon directly involved in Daisy's care. 'Any news on that front?'

'Got my bleeper,' Daisy said cheerfully, indicating the small device on the bedside table beside her.

Daisy's heart, despite her brightness, was severely damaged, functioning poorly and in urgent need of replacement. She was near the top of the recipient list for a transplant at the hospital and she carried the bleeper so the transplant team could reach her any time a suitably matched organ became available. 'It never leaves my side.' Her face stilled momentarily.

'Mr Grant says things have been a bit quiet lately. It's funny the way that makes you feel, isn't it? I mean lately, now that I'm hoping it might not be too long before I have the surgery, and no matter how much I want the operation, I still feel a bit relieved there aren't any spare hearts because it means that other people aren't suffering too much.'

'That's a common feeling,' murmured Annabel. Waiting for a donor heart was never easy because hoping for one meant there was always an element of guilt about the fact that another person had first to die. The transplant team included specialist counsellors who were skilled at helping recipients explore such issues and she felt it was a sign of their good work that Daisy felt able to voice her confusion so fluently. 'Want me to ask one of the team to pop up and chat with you?'

Daisy shook her head. 'I'm fine,' she said firmly. 'Being in here, there's just less to keep me distracted, I think. I go to see them every month anyway.'

'I've got clinics all day but I'll be up to see you when

they finish before you go tonight,' Annabel told her. She quickly explained to the younger doctors the changes she'd made to Daisy's treatment. 'How many admissions is that, then, these past six months?' she asked her SHO outside Daisy's room.

'Four.' Mark ran back through Daisy's notes, checking. 'Four plus that one time she only needed to stay a couple of hours.'

Annabel nodded. 'Better ECHO her again this afternoon,' she told her registrar, referring to a type of heart scan, similar to the sort used during pregnancy to see the baby. An ECHO would provide valuable information on both the size of Daisy's heart and the way it was functioning. She'd scanned her personally in clinic the day before but it would be useful to have a further measurement of how she was coping after twenty-four hours' intensive treatment.

With the lecture and with her clinics so busy that afternoon, she wouldn't have time to do the scan herself, but Hannah was a relatively senior registrar with two years of specialist training in cardiology behind her and she was skilled at the procedure. 'Just remind me you need to leave early from clinic later on so you can fit it in,' she instructed.

The rest of her ward round—M and J were her main wards but she had patients scattered throughout the four main medical wards, as well as two currently on transplant wards and three in Intensive Care—progressed smoothly but her patient load was currently very high and both she and Hannah—leaving the ward work to Mark—were still late getting down to Outpatients.

She neither expected nor wanted, and she certainly hadn't asked for, Luke's help with the session, and when she saw him ensconced in the examination room she usually used herself, she drew herself up sharply, thrown momentarily off balance by her body's sudden nervous, heart-skipping reaction to seeing him. 'What are you doing here?'

'Harry,' he responded blandly, meeting her shocked regard with frustrating equanimity. 'He thinks I should get my feet wet. He decided Outpatients would be a good place to start.'

Annabel felt like asking when he had started taking orders from anyone but himself, but, of course, that would have been deliberately provocative and since she was determined to avoid arguing with him she held her tongue. 'Fine,' she replied stiffly instead. 'Is there anything you'd like to tell me about any of my patients or have you taken them out of my hands completely?'

'Don't turn territorial on me, Annie.' The tightening around his mouth suggested he'd sensed her reaction even if she was doing her best to mask it. 'You're not under threat. The two men I've looked at so far have been general referrals to the hospital, not personal ones to your clinic or follow-ups. Believe me, I am aware of the basic principles of ethical medical practice.'

'Oh, I'm sure you know a list of them by heart,' she retorted with what she felt was creditable pleasantness, considering he'd just called her Annie again, taken over her office and, probably, at least a third of her clinic as well.

New referrals to the hospital for advice on management of both private and public system patients with heart disease made up a significant portion of their clinic workload. Those intended for particular consultants were allocated to them, of course, but patients with general referrals tended to be distributed evenly among the teams by the administrative staff.

Her own clinics were invariably overloaded, and in normal circumstances she'd have been grateful for help, but, knowing that help was coming from Luke, it made it more difficult for her to appreciate it.

Nevertheless, she managed a small smile. 'I'll just take the office next door,' she said sweetly, collecting herself, along with the stack of notes on the table nearest the door. The other room was smaller and, being internal with no windows to the outside, darker, but at least it wasn't opposite where she'd be able to see him whenever their doors were opened between patients. Besides, she refused to add to his entertainment by asserting her right to the room they were in now. 'If you've any questions, please, don't hesitate...'

He seemed to find the way she let the words trail off amusing. His mouth quirked. 'I won't,' he said quietly.

'Then I'll leave you to it.' The door behind her was still half-open but now she pulled it wide.

'When did you cut off your hair?'

She froze momentarily, then turned slowly back to him, one hand lifting self-consciously to the now almost brutally short, silky red strands behind her ear. Luke had liked her hair long. He'd loved grabbing great fiery handfuls and twisting their bodies in it until they were bound together.

The memory of the way he'd liked to make love to her like that brought hot colour surging up from her chest to her face.

She was used to herself with short hair now. She still had a photograph at the house of herself with it long, but these days the sight of her hair falling below her waist, the way she'd worn it in her years with Luke, invariably startled her. 'Six years ago,' she said thickly, meeting the calculating regard with which he watched her flush with as much insouciance as she could manage.

'Interesting.' Despite that, he sounded bored. 'And do

you dress like this regularly now, Annie, or is the big cover-up routine strictly for my benefit?'

Annabel, still flushing, pulled the lapels of her white coat together clumsily over her dress. It wasn't worth it, she decided numbly. It wasn't worth it, protesting about her name. Even if hearing him say 'Annie' grated across her nerves like slow sandpaper. 'I'm older,' she stated nervously, referring to his comment about her clothes. 'I prefer a more suitable hairstyle and clothes—'

'Not that much older.'

'When I was young I wore young clothes. Now I'm old—'

'You're still a young woman.'

She swallowed heavily. 'What I choose to wear is none of your business.'

He lifted one broad shoulder in a careless movement that seemed to her intensely male and very Luke. 'I didn't say it was,' he said coolly. 'I was simply curious about why a woman who loved cosmetics, tight sweaters and short skirts now turns up two days in a row with a bare face and wearing a shapeless dress down to her ankles.'

'I've work to do.' Her hands shaking now, she walked out quickly and pulled the door shut behind her.

It was deliberate, she thought sickly, stumbling into the office next door. Either for his own…sadistic amusement or out of some belated need for revenge for past sins, he was deliberately trying to unsettle her.

What was it he wanted from her? Did he want them to fight? Surely there'd been more than enough arguments during their marriage to mean he should be welcoming with relief her desperate attempts at a mature, professional co-existence?

CHAPTER THREE

'YOU don't mind, Annabel, about me putting Professor Geddes next door?' Wendy Dogherty, the charge nurse in Outpatients, came racing into Annabel's room before she'd even had a chance to sit down. 'I am sorry, I know you do like to work in there, only…well, we weren't expecting him.'

'It's all right, Wendy. I don't mind.' Annabel excused herself the lie because to admit anything else would have worried Wendy even more, and it already looked as if Luke's arrival had sent the normally composed nurse into something of a tail-spin. She could understand that. Luke had done something similar to her for years. He was still doing it now. 'He is the new big chief, after all. He should have the best room.'

'Well, that's what I thought—' But Wendy broke off, her pale complexion flushing. 'Well, the truth is, Annabel, we didn't know what to do with him. The girls are in a tizzy over him turning up. But he has been very good. He's not trying to be intimidating or anything and he asked to see only new referrals so he's not going to muck up your routine with anyone. I was going to put him in with Geoffrey Clancy but you're very full already this morning and you do have your lecture today so I thought you wouldn't mind the help.'

'That was thoughtful,' Annabel said carefully. 'Thank you.'

'One smile and their brains turn to drooling mush.' Wendy, it seemed, was still preoccupied, worrying about her nurses. 'I even felt a few heart flutters myself,' the nurse added breathlessly, 'and I'm nearly fifty! He's a knock-out all right. Does he have the same effect on you?'

'He hasn't smiled at me.' Annabel looked down at the notes she was holding. Rationally she knew Luke had never used his looks to the sort of advantage some other men might have, but emotionally she'd never been able to stay blasé about the way other women responded to him. It hadn't been easy, being married to a man who drew female attention so effortlessly. 'Are there many waiting?'

'I'll get Mary to show your first one in,' Wendy agreed in a distracted way, before bustling out.

At eleven it was customary for the team—doctors and nurses—to take a ten-minute break between patients to meet for morning tea. It was a chance to discuss cases they'd seen and bounce ideas off each other, but, her nerves on edge from her knowledge of Luke's proximity, Annabel checked with Hannah that there were no problems she wanted to discuss then carried her tea across to Geoffrey's team's side of the clinic.

'Hey!' Her colleague greeted her arrival with an easy grin, toasting her with his own tea, but his smile faded as he scanned her expression. 'What's up? Trouble?'

'I felt like a break with tradition,' she said smoothly, coming to sit on the corner of his desk. She looked down at the ECG he was studying. 'Busy?'

'Frantic.' He passed her the trace. 'What do you think?'

Annabel saw from the printed details at the top of the ECG that the tracing had come from a twenty-five-year-old male. 'Heart block in a young person,' she commented, referring to the fact that there was an obvious disruption between the electrical part of the heartbeat and the muscle's reaction. 'Sarcoid?'

'Spot on.' Geoffrey threw his pen onto the desk and

leaned back in his chair with a pleased air. 'He's had some palpitations and he's fainted twice, hence the referral here. I've organised for him to come in for an MRI to see if that gives us any more information,' he explained, referring to a type of scan which would give them good pictures of the structure of the heart. 'But his chest X-ray gave me the most likely answer this morning.'

Annabel glanced up at the X-ray on the board beside him and nodded. Sarcoidosis was a condition where organs, usually the lung but sometimes including the heart among others, became infiltrated with a hard, grainy substance. The cause was unknown but the flared deposits she could see in his X-ray were a characteristic finding. It was a chronic condition and it wasn't easy to treat. 'When are you inserting his pacemaker?'

'Tomorrow morning.' Insertion of a pacemaker could overcome problems with the heart rhythm—the most serious of which could lead to sudden death—caused by sarcoid in the heart. 'Obviously I've started steroids to try and prevent the heart becoming more involved,' Geoffrey added.

'You'll probably see him on the ward over the next day or two. I've sent him to J because they had a couple of spare beds. He seems a nice lad. He's a chef. He was telling me all about it. Hard work by the sound of it. He's thin, though, so I don't know what that says about his cooking. You'd think chefs would be fat, wouldn't you, if their food was any good?'

'I don't think there's any correlation.' Annabel took a few quick gulps of her tea. 'I'm sure there are lots of thin top chefs just as there must be fat bad chefs.'

'Sounds like me,' he said mournfully.

'You're not fat.' Annabel smiled. Geoffrey loved his food and his work commitments left him little time for exercise, but he wasn't alarmingly overweight. 'Geoffrey, you're just…pleasantly rounded.'

'*Rounded?*' He laughed then. 'Annabel, you're terrible for my ego. You know very well I was joking. All I meant was I can't cook. There's nothing wrong with my physique.'

'Of course there isn't,' she said quickly, too quickly perhaps because he promptly looked offended.

'I'm just short for my weight,' he protested.

'I'm leaving,' Annabel declared with a smile. She slid off his desk. 'I'm going to put my foot in it again if I say anything more.'

'Don't leave me.' His expression promptly turned back to mournful again and he made a playful grab for her arm and caught her wrist. 'Annabel, stay.' There was a brief knock at the door. Annabel heard it and stiffened, but Geoffrey seemed not to. 'You know I only eat to compensate for being lonely,' he teased. 'If you'd only agree to marry me—' He broke off, his expression dissolving into a grin as the door swung open to reveal Luke standing there.

Annabel froze but Geoffrey seemed unfazed. 'Ah, the great professor,' he said with a laugh. 'Come in. Come in. I was hoping to catch up with you this morning.' Geoffrey dropped Annabel's wrist and went to greet Luke. 'Geoffrey Clancy. If I hadn't seen you this morning I'd have come looking for you this afternoon to introduce myself. It's an honour to meet you. I've read so much of your Harvard work I almost feel as if I know you already.'

'Luke Geddes.' Annabel felt Luke's eyes briefly on her as he responded to the introduction. 'I'm interrupting.'

'You're not. You're not.' Annabel looked up in time to see Geoffrey make a slightly sheepish gesture towards her and she stood silently by as the two men shook hands. 'Come in. Annabel and I were just fooling around.'

'I did knock.' Luke's voice was calmly polite despite the cool green regard that swung to Annabel. 'You were pre-occupied.'

'Annabel has that effect on me.' Geoffrey gave one of his wry shrugs. 'Welcome to St Peter's, Luke. We're all still astounded at our luck in coaxing you here, but I imagine you've been told that often enough already. I've been away in Bristol, otherwise I'd have been back in time for the reception last night. How are you settling in?'

'Well.' Luke's gaze tracked between the two of them in a way that left Annabel in no doubt about what he was thinking. 'Geoffrey, did I just overhear you asking Annabel—?'

'Out of work already?' Annabel interrupted abruptly, preventing him from finishing his question. Ignoring the startled look her bald interjection provoked from Geoffrey, she rushed on, 'If you have, I'm sure Geoffrey has plenty of referrals you could see. He won't mind up giving a few. Swapping between us all is probably the most efficient way of building up your own list.'

Geoffrey looked bemused. 'Well, I don't—' he began uncertainly, but Annabel cut him off, more gently this time than she'd cut off her ex-husband.

'Professor Geddes wanted to start right in at the deep end,' she explained. 'He's already seen some of the general referrals on my list. You don't mind him seeing some of yours, do you, Geoffrey?'

'Not at all,' Geoffrey blustered, beginning to look a little less confused now, although the look he sent Annabel was frankly questioning. 'I mean, if you just ask Wendy,' he said to Luke, his gaze swinging back to him, 'she'll pass on all you need. Help yourself. I'd appreciate the help.'

'Thanks. And thank you, Annabel.' Luke looked thoughtful and she saw her intervention had raised his curiosity. 'Obviously I'm going to be able to rely on you to smooth over my transition here.' But his steady gaze said something far less polite to her. 'However, I have a pre-lunch meeting now through until lunch.'

'Lucky you,' Annabel replied evenly, holding herself stiffly to stop herself flinching from him when, with a brief nod to Geoffrey, Luke spun on his heel and walked out.

'Annabel…?' Geoffrey still looked puzzled. 'What was that all about? Am I missing something?'

'I was angry with him for eavesdropping,' she said defensively.

'Eavesdropping?' Geoffrey's spectacles had slipped down his nose and he pushed them up with his forefinger. 'But I don't think he was. He was only asking about what he must have heard me saying when he opened the door.'

'He had no right to ask about it.'

'But he's head of staff now. It makes sense he might be curious about us.'

'He has no right to be,' she said.

'I think he got the message.' Geoffrey blinked at her again. 'In fact, the poor man probably didn't know what hit him. You spoke right over him. You seemed to be determined to go out of your way to make him look foolish.'

That was too much. 'And did he?'

He looked blank. 'What?'

'Look foolish?'

'Well, not really,' Geoffrey conceded. 'In fact, I thought he handled it rather well, considering—'

'How rude I was,' Annabel finished. 'Yes, I know.' She sighed. Despite her colleague's worry on behalf of Luke, she had the advantage of knowing that Luke had never in his entire charmed life ever looked, or been made to look, foolish. 'I'm sorry,' she said quietly. 'Please, forget that. He rubs me the wrong way.' She made clumsily for the door. 'Fingernails on a blackboard stuff. I have to get back to work.'

Hannah was both senior enough and skilled enough to be able to see and assess patients and arrange investigations and treatment independently, in line with what she knew to be Annabel's own preferences, but when she wanted advice she always asked and at the end of each clinic they held a short session where they discussed the cases she'd seen.

This time, since Annabel had spent longer at morning tea than she'd intended and, despite Luke's earlier help, her clinic ran over time. As soon as she'd finished going over Hannah's case load she had to run to make it to the post-graduate seminar room in time to start her lecture.

The talk was a regular weekly session and was generally well attended by the hospital's medical, nursing and general staff, as well as medical students visiting St Peter's from the Free. The consultants tended to take it in turns with outside experts to deliver the lectures, which were carefully tailored to be of interest to all health professionals, rather than being aimed strictly at doctors.

Harry normally acted as the master of proceedings but when Annabel rushed into the hall it wasn't Harry's reassuring face she saw, waiting for her down the front, ready to introduce her, but Luke's distinctly unreassuring one.

'I see six years haven't been long enough for you to learn the simple courtesy of punctuality,' he murmured.

Annabel, despite conceding that she had once had a problem with getting anywhere on time, now considered herself an extremely punctual person, and she found his observation offensive. She drew herself up stiffly, determined not to let him guess her reaction. 'What have you done with Harry?'

'I haven't eaten him, if that's what you're worried about,' he said neutrally. 'Does this speech of yours have a title?'

'Current thinking on the role of infection in cardiac disease,' she said jerkily. 'Shouldn't you have read the title, before usurping poor Harry?'

'Just keep it short.' He sent her an impatient look on his way to the lectern. 'And to the point, if that's at all possible.'

As soon as he'd said that, Annabel began steeling herself for a terse introduction, and as he turned on the microphone and moved to speak she caught her breath, wondering what she was in for.

'Ladies and gentlemen, welcome to this afternoon's Dean's lecture, where you'll hear about current thinking in the role of infection in heart disease.' He spent a few moments introducing himself and explaining his new role as head of medicine, and then he turned slightly towards her. 'I have the pleasure today of introducing St Peter's youngest, yet also one of its most distinguished, widely admired and well-regarded physicians, Dr Annabel Stuart.'

Annabel, enormously startled by the unexpected generosity of his introduction and the applause his words provoked, managed a weak smile on her way to change places with him at the lectern. 'You didn't have to go overboard,' she murmured, waiting for the applause to die.

'Live up to it,' he commanded softly, before leaving her to her speech.

Annabel had no fears about public speaking. She was accustomed to teaching as her years of medical training and her job here at St Peter's involved lecturing to both junior doctors and medical students. But knowing Luke was there, knowing he'd be critically appraising her every word and movement, it made her nervous where normally she'd have been briskly confident, and for once she had to work hard at her presentation.

'When I was a doctor in training we treated peptic ulcers with either acid-reducing medication or complicated surgery,' she began, shakily at first but more strongly once her fascination for the topic came to dominate her anxiety about Luke's presence. 'These days, since the discovery that most ulcers are caused by an infection, the vast majority of sufferers are treated with antibiotics. Could it be that in ten years from now we'll be treating coronary artery diseases the same way?'

The topic was fascinating. Recent studies had led to interest in the possible dramatic role that bacteria, including the same organism implicated in causing stomach ulcers, might play in the development of coronary vessel disease or hardening of the arteries. If the results were confirmed in more thorough, extensive studies, there had to be a possibility that future treatment of heart disease might involve antibiotics rather than the powerful drugs and invasive surgery they used now.

'Although obviously these are very early days,' she reminded her audience as she drew her talk to a close. 'But I think you'll agree that the potential, if this work is proved, is awe-inspiring.'

She smiled her thanks at the round of applause which concluded her speech, then stood back, flushing slightly at the brief, approving look Luke sent her before he came forward to field what looked like dozens of questions from the floor.

'I'm going to take shameless advantage of my role as convenor to slip in one question of my own, Annabel,' he said mildly. 'I'm concerned that if this research is proved it might mean we cardiologists have no job to come to.' The observation provoked a murmur of amusement from the audience. 'Will the patients of the future with heart disease simply pick up a prescription from a GP, without ever needing further referral?'

'You may be right about our jobs disappearing.' Conscious both of their audience and her body's nervously heated reaction as she was forced to move closer to him to reach the microphone, Annabel lifted her shoulders, taking care not to look at him directly lest he saw how he was flustering her. 'But I don't expect many cardiologists will object to retiring a few years earlier than we might otherwise if it's for the greater good of humanity.'

The question-and-answer session continued up until the end of the hour when Luke smoothly thanked her for her talk and drew the lecture to a close.

'I have another session in Outpatients now,' Annabel told him as they drew away from the lectern. 'It's my fortnightly specialist cardiomyopathy clinic so you might find it interesting.' The diagnosis, treatment and understanding of diseases of the heart muscle was one of her own—as well as Luke's—special areas of interest and expertise. True, she hadn't welcomed his assistance that morning but after his professionalism this past hour she found herself in a more peaceable state of mind. 'You're welcome to join me if you're interested.'

'What's this, Annie?' Her ex-husband's very green eyes narrowed at her. 'This morning spitting and now smiling? You are a contrary girl. Or have you decided to call a truce?'

'We don't need a truce, Luke.' She let his taunting pass, determined not to allow him to provoke her again. 'I bear no ill feeling towards you,' she revealed evenly. 'Perhaps we'll never be able to be friends, but we can both be adult about this. There needn't be any impediment to us working well together.'

'You bear no ill feelings towards me.' Her ex-husband's regard turned thoughtful. 'That's an intriguing way of putting it, considering I've always assumed our separation was entirely mutually agreed.'

Annabel felt her face heat. 'Just because you assumed that, it doesn't mean it was true,' she said huskily. 'And what I meant was that I bear no ill feeling about you coming back. You have a perfect right to work wherever you want in the world.'

His brows drew together. 'I don't need your permission, Annabel.'

'I didn't say you did,' she retorted. She forced a faint smile in an attempt to take some of the sharpness out of her tone. 'I'm just trying to reassure you that I can put aside the pain of the past if you meet me halfway and stop bringing it up.'

Luke still frowned at her. 'Are you talking metaphorically or are you actually saying you found our divorce painful?'

'Of course I found it painful.' Unlike him, clearly. Until the actual moment he'd walked out on her, despite the arguments they'd been having, it had never occurred to her that he might leave. She'd—ludicrously—assumed their vows would hold them together for ever, regardless of what she'd thought of as their temporary difficulties. She hadn't properly realised then that love, outside the unconditional love a parent gave, rarely lasted. She hadn't known that it could be destroyed or so easily driven away.

But that night, when he'd packed a case then walked out to his car, she'd known, shockingly and immediately, that their marriage had been over. Luke hadn't been a man who'd made idle threats. When he'd quietly wished her well with her life and closed the door behind himself, the finality of the gesture had been absolute.

'Oh, yes,' she said huskily. 'I found it very painful.' It had taken her years to recover, and only recently had she begun to realise that by leaving when he had he'd done the best possible thing for both of them. Any longer and the damage he'd inflicted might have been permanent. 'I thought I'd never stop crying.'

'Clearly you did.'

'Clearly,' she agreed. 'You left on the Friday night and I had to be at work on the Monday. I had to pick myself up and get on with living my life.' She spread her arms, refusing to feel guilty about the defensive way she was downplaying the extent of the grief she'd suffered. 'As you see, here I am.'

'Happy?'

'Of course.' She frowned at the doubt in his tone. '*Very* happy,' she stressed. 'I've never been more content. I have a lovely home, I enjoy my work and my life is very pleasant.'

'Including a new fiancé?' he asked. 'Did you accept Clancy's proposal this morning?'

'I'm fond of Geoffrey.' She found herself avoiding answering his demand directly. 'He's a nice man. He's been good to me.'

Luke's eyes had narrowed and grown darker as she'd been speaking, and when she'd finished he said abruptly, 'Your life is *pleasant*.' The sudden harshness of his tone startled her. 'You're *content*,' he continued, equally scathingly. 'Clancy's a *nice* man. He's been *good* to you. You're *fond* of him. My God, Annie. You used to have passion and fire to match your hair, but look at yourself now and listen to what you're saying. What the hell's happened to you?'

Clearly—*thankfully*—not expecting any answer, he simply sent her a searching look then turned away from her and stalked out of the theatre, leaving her staring after him open-mouthed with bewilderment as to why her simple little remarks could have provoked such a strange reaction.

Annabel lifted a trembling hand to the hair he'd referred to so violently. Never mind what had happened to her, she thought dazedly. What had suddenly got into *him*?

CHAPTER FOUR

DESPITE Annabel's invitation, Luke didn't turn up to her clinic that afternoon and she heard from Geoffrey later that he'd been in a meeting with representatives from the department of surgery.

Daisy Miller, when she called in to see her on her ward round the next morning, looked cheerful. 'How was the movie?' asked Annabel.

'Great.' Daisy beamed. 'Well, from what I remember. I was too excited about all the famous people in the audience to notice much. And I was back on time,' she told her, dimpling a little when Annabel's registrar rolled her eyes tellingly. 'Well, maybe twenty minutes late, but that's all. And I'm in good shape today, Dr Stuart. I promise. My breathing's almost normal this morning and my heart's been fine. At least as fine as it ever is. I hardly even feel tired after last night and I haven't had any real problems since Monday. Can I go home?'

'Let's have a look at you.' Annabel examined her heart, the back of her chest then the pulsation level in one of the veins in her neck—the height of the pulsation gave her an indication of Daisy's fluid levels.

'Your ECHO yesterday wasn't as good as I was hoping it was going to be,' she conceded when she'd finished. One of the key indices they examined when they did the scan was the percentage of blood inside the heart's left ventricle ejected at each beat, and Daisy's result yesterday had shown a decline from the last time she'd been in hospital. 'Your ejection fraction's dropped again,' she told her patient, going through the figures since Daisy's understanding of her disease was intelligent and advanced. 'But you're not looking too bad so I suppose I'm happy for you to leave us.'

She smiled at Daisy's delighted whoop. 'Why so keen? What have you got planned?' She remembered that Daisy was dating a professional footballer. 'Another night out with the man with the great body, is it?'

'Clubbing tonight if I can convince him, and I said I'd come and see him play on Saturday,' Daisy revealed. 'I haven't seen him playing before, not properly, and it's a big game.'

'Have fun.' Annabel glanced over the chart her registrar had picked up for her to inspect. 'Your blood pressure's good. Oh, I had a word with Tony Grant last night,' she added, referring to Daisy's transplant surgeon. 'He said he'd be in first thing to say hello so you'd better wait around to see him before you go. I'm surprised he's not been in already. The surgeons are normally up and about round here by seven.'

'He did a transplant last night,' Daisy told her. 'He's probably slept in.'

'Did he?' Annabel raised her brows at her juniors, surprised she'd not heard anything about it. Normally word of such events got around the hospital fairly quickly. 'Who did they do?'

'Daniel McEanor,' Mark, her SHO, told her.

Annabel nodded. Daniel wasn't one of her patients but the consultants at St Peter's conferred frequently about their patients at case conferences and she'd been on call several times when Daniel had been admitted so she knew him fairly well. A nine-year-old with heart and lung complications secondary to a congenital heart condition, he'd been on home oxygen therapy, awaiting a heart and lung transplant for over a year, and critically ill in Intensive Care with both heart and lung failure at St Peter's for a week.

Annabel said her farewells to Daisy and organised for her to come to see her in Outpatients for a follow-up ECHO the following week. Outside in the corridor, she asked her registrar about Daniel's surgery.

'He's still touch and go, apparently,' Hannah told her gingerly. She waggled her hand in the air in a demonstration of the delicacy of the situation. 'Danny was already very ill before they started. It was a difficult operation, then they had trouble starting the heart and they had difficulties pacing it post-op. Without Danny in what passes for him as peak condition, it can't have been easy.'

'They couldn't have denied him the chance,' Annabel said quietly, blinking quickly.

She understood the dilemma the transplant team must have faced once a suitable heart size and tissue match for Danny had become available. In an ideal world precious, very scarce hearts would only be transplanted into people with highly realistic chances of survival but the reality was that it wasn't easy to veto critically unwell patients.

Children, particularly, were difficult to turn down when the potential benefits were so clear. She'd seen patients who'd otherwise have died within hours granted years of new life by the sudden availability of a transplant. With a child of Danny's age it would have been extraordinarily difficult to deny him that same chance, however slim the odds might have seemed of him surviving.

She finished her round just before nine then headed for her office. For three Wednesday mornings out of every four she held a clinic at St Joseph's, one of the outlying district hospitals affiliated to St Peter's, but today she was free to spend the three hours on administrative work and paperwork.

Her bleeper sounded as she got to her office and she answered it, expecting it to be Hannah about someone they'd inadvertently missed on the ward round, but her insides tightened when Luke answered.

'Annie, I was on call overnight,' he told her briskly, sounding as if he was in a hurry. 'I know we don't usually take cold referrals from GPs but I accepted an admission from a local one for a twenty-three-year-old woman with chest pain because he was convinced she's having a heart attack. She's arriving now on M and the nurses are getting her on a trolley and doing an ECG. I know you're on call for today so I'm letting you know out of courtesy, but I'm on the ward so I'll see her—'

'I'm free,' Annabel said quickly. 'I'll come and see her with you.' The chance of a twenty-three-year-old woman having a heart attack was so remote she suspected the woman's pain was more likely to be secondary to a muscle strain or indigestion, but it could be an embolism, a blood clot on her lungs, so she might still require immediate treatment.

When she ran onto M, one of the nurses at the main desk directed her to the first side room. The room was crowded. Two nurses were drawing up drugs and organising oxygen and fixing monitor leads to their patient's chest, and Luke was inserting an intravenous line into the fair-haired, pale and very distressed-looking young woman.

Luke looked up briefly when Annabel came in and nodded her towards the completed ECG now sitting on top of the portable machine just inside the door. 'Tamsin, this is Annabel Stuart, one of the other heart doctors who works with me,' he said briskly as he slid his venflon into place. 'Annabel, this is Tamsin Winston and her baby, George. Tamsin started getting severe left-sided chest and arm and back pain two hours ago. Her breathing is fine but she feels sick and she's vomited once.'

'Hello, Tamsin.' Annabel did her best to keep her smile reassuring as she reached for the cardiogram. 'What a lovely baby,' she murmured, one eye on the sleeping infant in a cot beside the bed, the other on the heart monitor above the bed. She read the ECG quickly, followed by the GP's letter beneath it, then put both away and reached urgently for her stethoscope to examine Tamsin's chest. 'How old is he?'

Tamsin shifted the oxygen mask Luke had obviously prescribed for her. 'Nine days,' she gasped.

Annabel adjusted the mask back into place. 'He's gorgeous.' She bent over Tamsin and put her stethoscope to her chest. 'You must be very proud.'

She checked Tamsin's heart and lungs then lifted her head. Luke was instilling a syringe full of clear fluid into the line he'd inserted. The nurse assisting him held up a glass ampoule for him to check and Annabel saw he was giving their patient morphine.

'Heart sounds normal,' she told Luke crisply. 'No extra sounds. Chest clear.' She looked up at the monitor recording Tamsin's heart rhythm and paled. VT, or ventricular tachycardia, was an abnormal rhythm that could quickly lead to cardiac arrest. 'Luke, VT on the monitor.'

Luke followed her eyes and nodded. 'Unsustained,' he said quietly, when the rhythm resolved on its own a few seconds later. 'This should help the pain,' he told Tamsin, his expression revealing none of the concern Annabel was feeling as he looked at their patient. 'It should work quickly. I've given you something for your nausea as well.'

'I'm feeling a little better already.' Tamsin spoke hoarsely, her voice muffled a little by her mask.

A radiographer began pushing her X-ray machine into

the room to take a chest X-ray, and at the same time the nurse who'd given Annabel directions put her head around the door. 'I finally managed to get hold of your husband and he's leaving work now,' she told Tamsin. 'He'll be here in about twenty minutes.'

Annabel, still very worried about Tamsin's heart rhythm, tore her eyes away from her monitor long enough to see the other woman's nod of acknowledgement. She was still pale and unwell-looking but Annabel thought her face looked a little less strained and she put that down to the morphine beginning to take effect.

Luke took the shield the radiographer offered him, clearly intending to stay in the room while the X-ray was taken, but he directed Annabel, along with the two nurses, outside onto the ward away from the radiation.

'What do you think it is?' the younger of the two nurses asked Annabel. 'I haven't seen the ECG yet. Is it an embolism?'

'Her GP was right about her having a heart attack.' Annabel had brought the ECG out with her and she passed it to her to study.

'What?' The other woman looked shocked. 'At twenty-three?'

'Rare but not unknown in the first two weeks after giving birth,' Annabel explained. She reached for the telephone on the wall outside the room. 'It's probably secondary to damage to one of the arteries supplying her heart. Luke will want to do an angio,' she added, referring to a test where contrast was injected into the vessels around the heart so they could visualise them. 'Depending on what that shows, she'll probably need bypass surgery this morning.'

When X-Ray answered she warned them they'd be needing an urgent angio and requested porters to help transfer their patient. She bleeped the on-call surgeon for the day and warned him of Tamsin's condition and the possibility that they'd need to refer her for emergency surgery.

'Call me, Annabel, as soon as you get the pictures,' he told her briskly. 'I'll come straight down and see them. I'm in Theatres now so I'll let the charge nurse and duty anaesthetist know there's a chance we're going to have to operate.'

In Tamsin's room, Luke had obviously just finished explaining what he suspected was happening with her because Tamsin looked stunned. 'What happens for heart attacks?' she gasped hoarsely. 'Pills? Or will I have to have an operation?'

Luke said, 'We'll know for sure after the heart X-rays. But there is a chance you'll need an operation today, yes.'

Perhaps sensing his mother's distress, Tamsin's baby had started to cry. Annabel picked him up in his little blanket and rocked him slightly, murmuring words of comfort, and thankfully he quietened. Luke was busy changing Tamsin's infusion but when Annabel, who'd been watching the monitor, made a small sound he glanced up, registered the briefly unstable rhythm again and met her eyes for a tense second of mutual understanding. He left the drip and pulled Tamsin's bed out from the wall. 'Time to move,' he ordered.

'X-Ray's expecting us,' Annabel told him quickly as the nurses scrambled to help as he began pushing Tamsin's bed out of the cubicle. 'Porters should be on their way up. And I've spoken to Simon Rawlings,' she added, referring to the surgeon she'd contacted, hurrying to catch up with Luke and the nurses as they wheeled the bed along the ward. 'He'll come to X-Ray once we've got pictures.'

'Thanks.' They reached the foyer outside the ward. Luke punched in the code number that summoned an urgent lift then turned back to Annabel, his eyes briefly narrowing on the way she still held their patient's baby cradled against her chest. Unaccountably Annabel felt herself flushing, and she saw him note that before his eyes veered away from her as the lift chimed to indicate its arrival.

Fortunately the porters arrived at the same time to help. Annabel left the baby in the care of the nurse who was remaining on the ward. Two nurses came with them, one taking charge of the resuscitation trolley with its defibrillator and drugs in case Tamsin arrested in the lift or in the corridor, the other supervising the intravenous fluid Luke had started to keep her drip open.

A radiographer and one of the cardiac catheter nurses were waiting for them in X-Ray. Angiography was always performed in one of the sterile theatres in the specialist cardiac catheter suite attached to the department. All normal theatre precautions, such as special clothing and sterile equipment, were used.

Luke went to change into theatre gear but as the changing facilities were unisex, offering little concession to shyness, and since Annabel had no intention of either embarrassing herself or entertaining Luke by retreating childishly into the cramped privacy of a toilet or shower cubicle to change her clothes, she stayed outside deliberately, using the time to organise the paperwork and Tamsin's consent form while they waited for him to return.

Luke emerged just as Tamsin was being wheeled through into the theatre. Despite the urgency of the situation he looked calm and disturbingly attractive in the baggy theatre-style pants and jerkin and Annabel felt her pulse jerk. The green of the outfit intensified the colour of his eyes and the fit of the pants accentuated the muscled power of his thighs. She despised herself for being immediately and overwhelmingly aware of him, but she avoided the enquiring look he sent her, murmured something about having organised the consent form and fled back the way he'd just come to change into her own gear.

A few minutes later she hurried into the theatre in regulation baggy blue theatre smock and tied-waist pants, an elasticised paper hat covering her red hair. She tied her paper face mask over her nose and face as she walked.

Luke was already scrubbing and he sent her a brief, assessing look but she veered self-consciously away from him and headed for the rack of plastic-covered, lead-lined aprons by the door. Lifting one of the heavy aprons over her head—the garments were uncomfortable but vital for shielding them from the X-rays they'd been using—she walked over to Tamsin who was lying quietly on a trolley in the centre of the room. 'How's the pain now?'

'It's there in the background but nothing like before,' the younger woman said weakly. 'Is this going to hurt, Doctor?'

Annabel shook her head firmly. 'I'm going to inject a sedative into this needle in your arm,' she explained. She nodded her thanks when one of the X-ray nurses wheeled over a steel trolley containing the swabs, needle, syringe and medication she'd need.

'Professor Geddes is going to put the needle I talked about before into your thigh here and then he'll push a catheter up to the arteries around your heart, but he'll use local anaesthetic first so that bit won't hurt at all. You'll feel quite sleepy. You'll be awake and you'll be able to watch the pictures of your heart on the television screen up here above your bed.' She indicated the monitor, one of three in the room. 'But you'll probably find you don't remember anything about this afterwards.'

Luke worked very fast. Catheterising the heart arteries wasn't one of Annabel's special areas of skill, although she was quite capable of carrying out the procedure in an emergency if required, as now when there was no radiology doctor immediately available, but Luke's obvious confidence and the smooth fluency of his technique was impressive.

He threaded his catheter up from Tamsin's groin through her heart and injected dye through each of the arteries supplying her heart in turn. Annabel talked Tamsin through the procedure and the pictures on the monitor above her head. When the problem became clear she looked quickly at Luke, acknowledged his nod, then motioned for a nurse to come and sit in her place.

The surgeon answered his bleeper immediately. 'Simon, it's Annabel Stuart,' she said urgently. 'She's dissected her left anterior descending,' she explained, meaning that the lining of the artery supplying part of Tamsin's heart had torn so that blood was now flowing down uselessly inside the wall of the vessel rather than though its central lumen. The condition was critical because, firstly, it meant that insufficient blood was reaching the heart muscle to keep it alive, hence Tamsin's heart attack, and, secondly, because the vessel could rupture at any moment and that would be fatal.

'Two minutes,' Simon told her tightly.

He was quicker than that and as soon as he saw the pictures he agreed to take Tamsin immediately to Theatre. Tamsin was drowsy from her pain relief and sedation but she seemed to understand the surgeon's explanation. As soon as Luke had withdrawn his catheter and applied pressure to her wound, the theatre porters transferred her to a theatre trolley and began wheeling her away.

'I'll explain to Tamsin's husband and bring him up to Theatres,' Annabel told Luke, leaving him and the nurses to accompany Tamsin. 'M ward's just rung to say he's waiting on the ward.'

Craig Winston, waiting in Tamsin's room on M, looked very young and obviously distraught. 'A heart attack?' he echoed thickly. '*A heart attack?* But Tamsin's twenty-three. No one in her family's ever had heart trouble. How could this happen?'

'It's rare but this sort of damage to a blood vessel can happen sometimes after having a baby.' Annabel hurried him ahead of her and towards the stairs, rather than waiting for the lift, in the hope that they'd be in time for him to see his wife for a few seconds before her surgery.

'But she was fine yesterday.'

Annabel sent him a sympathetic look as they rushed down the stairs. 'It's all happened very quickly. There's very rarely any warning with this condition. What's good is that she's made it to hospital in time to be treated.'

'This operation,' he said sickly as she opened the door and directed him out onto the lower floor. 'Is it open heart?'

Annabel nodded. 'Mr Rawlings will want to do bypass surgery and that's open-heart surgery, yes. He'll probably take a blood vessel from either Tamsin's arm, leg or chest and transplant it to replace the artery that's torn.'

She ushered him towards the main doors into Theatres. There were clean gowns on a hook outside and she grabbed one for herself and passed him one to cover his clothes. Tamsin and the nurse looking after her were just inside the main entrance, one of the theatre nurses still busy checking through the paperwork and confirming Tamsin's identity with the details on her hospital bracelet.

Craig rushed past Annabel to embrace his wife and the couple had a few moments together before Tamsin had to be transferred into the operating theatre. Annabel put her arm around Craig's back, showed him gently through to the waiting area and sat with him for a little while, answering his questions.

When he seemed marginally more settled she fetched him a pot of tea from the adjacent kitchen and arranged for one of the theatre receptionists to keep a check on him and let Simon Rawlings know he was waiting so he could talk to him at the end of the operation.

She ran back downstairs to X-Ray, intent now on exchanging her theatre clothes for her normal clothes again, intending to make good use of the hour she still had left by getting some of her paperwork done. She was almost back at the changing room when one of the department's radiologists called out to her from his office at the far end of the hall.

'Annabel, glad I caught you,' he said quickly. 'Have you still got those films you mentioned at the meeting last week? If you have, I wouldn't mind having a look at them. I wanted to make copies for teaching.'

'I'll drop them into your office in the morning,' Annabel promised, pausing with her hand on the door. 'The folder's on my desk at home.' The X-rays were copies of those from a baby she'd been asked to see a month earlier who had been born with *situs inversus* meaning his heart and abdominal organs were swapped around in his chest and abdomen so that his heart was on the right side of his chest instead of his left and his liver was on the left side instead of the right.

The other doctor lifted his hand in acknowledgement, before disappearing back into his office, and Annabel pushed the changing-room door open and kicked off the clogs she'd been wearing. Happily the baby with the *situs inversus* had appeared perfectly well, and was in no need of any treatment. The unusual switch had only been picked up when the delivering obstetrician had been worried that the baby's heart sounds were so indistinct—

'Oh.' She brought herself up sharply, meeting Luke's

sanguine expression with shock. He was almost dressed, thank God, and buttoning his shirt with brisk haste, although not before she'd caught a glimpse of a disturbingly familiar broad chest, but still she registered the intimacy of catching him like this with startled dismay. 'I'll...wait outside. I was sure you'd be gone by now.'

'I was on call all night and I haven't had time to make it back to the hotel yet.' The sudden impatience of his regard suggested he found her shock irritating. 'I took a shower.' Only then did she register the damp darkness of his hair. 'For heaven's sake, Annabel, stop standing there like a nun and close the damn door. I'm decent. Even if I wasn't, you've seen me dressing often enough before.'

She had, just as she'd seen several of her colleagues in similar situations—they all invariably dressed after showering in the cubicle but such things as ties and jackets and shoes were generally left until the main room—but she was still, with Luke, finding the experience distressingly disconcerting. He lifted the collar of his shirt and threaded his tie around it, tied it immaculately, then ran a towel through his hair again, not even glancing her way, but still she stood, frozen, tensely aware of him.

'I'm supposed to be in a meeting with someone at Medical Staffing in ten minutes,' he said crisply. He balled the towel he'd been using then lobbed it effortlessly into the appropriate linen bag at the end of the room. 'Remind me again where the department is.'

'Just behind Rehabilitation,' she told him sharply.

His mouth compressed and she could sense his abrupt annoyance like a tangible haze around him. 'What have I done now?'

'Nothing.' She looked away. 'Nothing. I'm sorry.' She took in a quick, steadying breath. 'I'm just a bit...tense about Tamsin, I suppose. She's so…young. But I think she'll be all right now, don't you?'

'Simon Rawlings seems confident,' he affirmed, still looking impatient. 'The surgery should be fairly straight-forward. Annabel—'

'Medical Staffing is in a separate small prefab building just behind Rehab,' she interrupted quickly. 'It's well la-belled. You can't miss it.' She lowered her hands to the bulky hem of her jerkin then stopped. 'Don't let me delay you.'

He merely sent her a grim look and crouched to fasten his shoes, forcing her to acknowledge she'd been wrong about him being ready to leave. When he'd finished he simply stood slowly, folding his arms and looking at her without making any move towards leaving, and in the end, still foolishly holding onto her top yet unable to ignore him, Annabel was forced to look directly at him. 'What?'

'Do you have a problem?'

'You're not the only one who has to be somewhere in a hurry,' she replied stiffly. 'I would prefer it if I had a little privacy while I change into my clothes.'

His regard turned abruptly incredulous. 'You think I'm dallying so I can *peek* at you?'

'Of course not.' The suggestion was as absurd as he made it sound. He'd seen her naked hundreds of times, thousands possibly. She knew the shape of her body could hold no fascination for him.

'Because frankly, Annabel, I'm not that desperate—'

'I believe you,' she interrupted. A man like Luke would never have been desperate. A man who only had to walk into a room to have every woman in the place turn to look at him didn't even know the meaning of the word. The thought had never occurred to her. If she had suspected him of lingering, his motivation would have been clear to her. To make her self-conscious, certainly. Embarrassed, of course. Unbalanced, definitely.

Just as he was doing all those things by not leaving now. Turning her back on him, she stalked in her stockinged feet to her locker and, when he still didn't budge, hauled the metal door open.

'This is ridiculous,' she pointed out stiffly, gathering up her long skirt, blouse, jacket and shoes, her annoyance making her careless—despite the hours she spent ironing— of creasing. 'This whole situation is completely ridiculous. Why is it impossible to have a normal, simple conversation with you without it turning into an argument? Why does my making a simple little request for a little bit of privacy have to turn into some grand drama?'

She hugged her clothes against her and made for the shower cubicle herself. Regardless of how foolish scrambling around dressing in there was going to make her feel, it felt, right then, like a far lesser evil than trying to dress in front of him.

But he caught her arm as she stalked past him and sheer shock, as much as force, brought her swinging around to face him, the clothes she'd been clutching dropping soundlessly away from her to the tiled floor.

'Why are you getting so uptight about something as trivial as me maybe catching you in a bra?' he demanded. 'Have you turned just plain irrational, Annie, or do you think the sight of you in whatever sexy little scrap you've got on under that thing will drive me wild? Is that what you think? You think that after a divorce and six years you can still turn me on?'

'I'd slit my throat rather than try,' she snapped, hateful awareness of his strength and of the warm, freshly showered scent of his body sending her senses spinning and her temper flaring. 'I don't think anything, I just want you out of here.' But her struggles were just bringing her closer against the hardness of his body. 'How dare you… *manhandle* me, you madman? If you don't let me go right now, and I mean right, *right* now, I swear I'll scream the entire roof of this hospital down.'

'No, you won't. You're too petrified someone will catch us together.' It was true, although she hadn't realised it until then, but she opened her mouth anyway to frighten him. To her utter and absolute outrage, Luke calmly put his hand over her mouth and lifted her off the floor, holding her effortlessly against him with his other arm despite her best attempts at furious resistance. 'And I promise you I'd make it look good,' he murmured, his mouth warm against her ear, his tone so smooth and reasonable she knew the threat was real.

'You're suffocating me,' she yelled fiercely, although against his hand it only came out as a muffled rumble. 'I can't breathe.'

'That's because you're hyperventilating,' he chided, rocking her slightly. 'You always hyperventilate when you're wild. Stop kicking me. You're not hurting and you'll only break your toes. I'm not going to touch you. Not unless you keep fighting.'

When she still, panicking, fought him, he brought his mouth so close to her ear that the heat of his breath on her skin sent shocks tingling across her cheeks to her own mouth.

'Annie, be calm or you *will* turn me on and, I promise you, neither of us wants that to happen. Breathe slowly and quietly. Prove to me you're going to be sensible and I'll let you go.'

Annabel went rigid. Disgust, she told herself. Appalled, sickened, disgust. But, given her stricken awareness of the powerful muscles of Luke's thighs and stomach against her lower back and legs, it was clear she had no choice but to give in to him. She wasn't a midget but Luke was a good six inches taller and many stones heavier and she'd been in his arms often enough to know she would never get away unless he allowed it.

The difference, of course, was that in the past she'd found the contrast in their sizes and strength sexually exciting so that her struggles had always been fake. Now, though, she held her body still and stiff and after a few heated, fiery seconds he put her down.

'Brute,' she accused, spinning about, her eyes narrowing to slits. 'Caveman. Some things never change—'

'Some things change far too much,' he said abruptly. 'But now at least you can satisfy my curiosity on one of your most memorable characteristics…' Before she could guess what he was going to do, he grabbed the bottom of her smock and jerked it, along with the vest she wore under it, up and completely over her head. 'Ah, Annie,' he said, his tone odd, almost despairing as he studied her sensibly covered breasts. 'Is this Clancy's doing? Is the man a lunatic?'

'*Geoffrey*,' Annabel said through gritted teeth, retrieving the jerkin and vest from the floor where he'd discarded them and clutching them to her chest fiercely, 'doesn't choose my underwear.'

The Annie *Geddes* Luke had known might have loved daring, low-cut lace and silk, bought for her own sensual pleasure as much as to drive her husband out of his mind, but Annabel *Stuart*'s life was too busy for hand-washing delicates, and she preferred beige, supportive, nylon, department-store styles because they were strong, comfortable and unlikely to fall to shreds the instant they saw the inside of a washing machine.

The fierce blush she felt at his critical inspection was

nothing to do with remembering the erotic pleasure of choosing the fripperies then having him slowly uncover her again, and certainly nothing to do with the embarrassment she was conscious of about being caught wearing such an unflattering garment, but merely fury at him exposing her. 'Not all men are Neanderthals,' she informed him haughtily.

'If you believe that, you don't understand us,' Luke said softly, his eyes intent on the shape of her behind the protection of the clothes she clutched. 'Underneath, we all are.' Tugging the jerkin and vest away from her with no more effort than he'd taken it away from her minutes before, he fastened a thumb around the top of each thick beige cup and dragged the fabric down brutally so it bunched at her midriff, pushing up her rose-tipped breasts, leaving them high and bare and achingly, betrayingly aroused.

For one brief, shattering moment Luke's glittering gaze burned into her, but then he lowered his head. 'The Neanderthal in me has always preferred you like this,' he growled, lifting her up to him.

CHAPTER FIVE

WEDNESDAYS were invariably busy for Annabel. Even on the one day of the month when she had administrative time instead of a clinic in the morning, she was on call for the hospital and for all emergency admissions for the twenty-four hours starting at nine in the morning.

At twelve she had either journal club or a junior doctor teaching session, each held fortnightly on a rotating basis, immediately followed by her busiest clinic of the week. Since that, despite her best efforts to eliminate waiting times for her patients, invariably ran over time, it was generally after seven before she made it to the wards for her usual evening ward round.

Tonight, thankfully, given the distracted state of her mind and the fact that she was on call for emergencies and medical admissions to the hospital all night, the wards seemed relatively quiet.

Tamsin Winston was transferred directly from Theatres to the surgical intensive care unit. The operation had gone well, Simon Rawlings had told her when he'd bleeped her afterwards, and he'd seemed very pleased with the results. From the unit Tamsin would be transferred to one of the surgical wards in a day or two under Simon's care so, although Annabel intended keeping in contact with Tamsin to see how she was getting on, she was no longer her patient.

Hannah told Annabel that apart from what sounded like a relatively straightforward transfer from another hospital of one of her own patients who'd been admitted in heart failure they weren't expecting any other admissions. 'Hopefully, I won't have to call you in again,' the registrar said ruefully with a grimace. 'Remember last week?'

Annabel made a casual gesture. The last night they'd been on call had been extraordinarily busy and they'd both been up all night, looking after two acute admissions and one very ill inpatient, Danny McEanor, the young boy who'd just had his heart transplant.

'I'm going to visit Tamsin then Danny in the unit before I leave. After that I'll be at home if you need me,' she told the registrar. At St Peter's on-call registrars stayed at the hospital while consultants made themselves available, if needed, from home. 'Tony Grant says Danny's looking marginally better this evening. He's having his first post-op heart biopsy tomorrow to check for rejection but they're much happier with his progress now.'

They were lucky at St Peter's in that on-call duties weren't usually arduous. In her years as a junior doctor at the Free she'd grown used to chronically disturbed nights and getting by with little or no sleep, but these days it was unusual for her to need to return to the hospital after hours.

Not that she lived so far away that it was a trial to come back. The house she and Luke had moved into after their wedding was in a leafy part of Maida Vale, not far from St Peter's, so out of peak traffic times she could generally count on getting from her living room to her office door in less than ten minutes.

Fortunately, tonight, since she was having trouble concentrating, traffic was light and she made it home without incident. Still feeling strangely vague, as if her body and mind were operating on autopilot, she let herself in. She emptied a can of tomato soup into a pan and turned on the heat to low, put bread in the electric toaster, then went upstairs and absently put water on for a bath.

In her bedroom she undressed slowly, letting her clothes slide to the floor in thoughtless disorder. Deliberately avoiding looking at the reflection of her face in the mirror, she meandered into the bathroom and climbed into the steaming water, slid down into it and tipped her head back so the warmth of the water lapped her forehead, submerging her hair and ears until she bent her knees and allowed her head to slide completely under.

Shock, she supposed when she came up again a few seconds later blinking and wet. That was what this dull, empty, strange feeling had to be. She was shocked.

Not that Luke had touched her—she'd never resisted him before and she understood that her attempts to do so today had inadvertently thrown him a challenge he hadn't been able to stand back from—and although she didn't like it she understood why her body had responded—simply because it always had—but what shocked her had been what had happened after that.

She'd never, in rage or calm, lashed out at anyone or anything before, and the fact that she could physically and violently strike Luke the way she had appalled her.

Not that her relationship with Luke—her *old* relationship with Luke—hadn't been physical. Because it had been passionately, sometimes primitively, physical. There'd even been nights, long, dizzying nights, when they'd deliberately driven each other to the edge of pain simply to increase the intensity of their pleasure. But he'd never, even by accident of his sheer size compared with hers, inside or outside bed, hurt her and she, too, had always been aware of boundaries she never breached, boundaries where they might have caused each other real harm.

Today, for the first time, she'd lost that control. When he'd lifted her, intent on her breasts, she'd swung her arm back then slammed her spread palm flat and hard with all her force across his face.

She'd seen the imprint of her fingers red against the abrupt pallor of his skin but Luke had barely flinched. He'd still held her but when she'd sworn at him to let her go he'd released her and stepped away from her, his expression stunned, his movements abruptly jerky and unnatural in contrast to his normal careless grace.

Wordlessly she'd pulled up her bra with trembling hands to cover herself. She'd retrieved her theatre top and hauled it on, but had left her clothes scattered across the floor where they'd fallen when he'd first grabbed her. Then she'd snatched her white coat and pulled open the main door to the room and run away from him.

She hadn't—thank God—seen him since. Harry had seemed to be expecting him at the journal club meeting but he hadn't come. In the afternoon she'd crept back down to the angio suite and retrieved her clothes—she'd been mortified to find them neatly folded on a chair rather than strewn across the room where she'd left them—and dressed again.

Now she didn't know what to do.

The sound of tapping at the glass panel in the front door downstairs as she was dressing after her bath didn't worry her. Her neighbours on both sides were elderly widows who occasionally called in on her in the evenings to invite her for cups of tea or to deliver mail they'd collected for her during the day as several of the medical journals she subscribed to were too large for the small mail vent in her door. Genuine visitors tended to ring the electric doorbell.

But, then, Luke knew how discordant the jangling of the bell sounded from inside. She knew as soon as she saw the broadness of the shape through the central patterned glass of the door that it was him, and when she swallowed jerkily and opened the door her eyes rose immediately, anxiously, to his cheek.

In her mind she'd expected to see redness or bruising at least the size of her hand, but there was nothing.

'It barely hurt,' he said quietly. 'You'd need a hammer to bruise me.'

'I was still expecting to see marks,' she answered dully. She stood back automatically to let him into the hall behind her. 'Luke, I'm sorry—'

'Don't be.' He barely looked at her, instead wandering about the neatly furnished living room to their right. 'I asked for it. You've redecorated.' He sounded tired. 'Tell me, does Clancy live here now?'

'No.' She lingered in the doorway, watching uneasily as he scanned the collection of framed photographs on the oak shelf above the gas fire. 'Geoffrey likes living south of the river,' she said huskily, when Luke picked up one of the photos. 'You're right, you did ask for it, but hitting you like that was still unforgivable.'

'I'm surprised Clancy hasn't adapted by now.' He made no comment on her apology. 'How long have you known him? It's eighteen months since you started at St Peter's, isn't it? Or did you know him before?'

'I met him during my registrar days at the hospital but we didn't become friends until I started this job.'

She was finding it hard to tear her gaze away from the photograph he still held of her and her father together after her graduation ceremony. Luke had taken the picture, she remembered. He'd probably picked it up because he'd recognised it. There'd been professional photographs taken, too, that day, photographs she hadn't been able to look at for a long time, but this was a snapshot of her father and her both looking so happy she hadn't been able to let it go.

It had been a beautiful, unseasonably warm London afternoon and after the formal part of the ceremony her father had taken her and Luke out to celebrate. She'd drunk too much champagne and she'd been dizzy and laughing, intoxicated as much with joy that after weeks of her pleading Luke had agreed to come with them as with the occasion and the alcohol itself.

But the afternoon didn't end there. After calmly taking that photograph of them together in the hotel grounds where they'd gone for a meal, then seeing her father into a cab, Luke finally—after almost a year of treating her fevered declarations of love and desire and her clumsy attempts to seduce him with brutal and detached amusement—gave in to her. He booked a room at the hotel, took her upstairs and quietly tore off her gown and dress.

When she eventually woke she was flushed and still dazed from the unexpected passion of his love-making and the disturbing, sweetly savage response he'd been able to draw from her previously untutored body. She knew herself to be utterly in love with him, yet she expected him to send her away. Instead, he covered her face with kisses and her body with roses and stunned her by telling her he wanted to marry her.

Nine weeks later, they were husband and wife. Her father, she knew, wasn't happy about the haste. He worried that she was too young, too new to her career and too obsessed with Luke, but at the same time he liked and trusted his future son-in-law, admired his academic achievements and desperately wanted grandchildren, so his objections had been slight and muted and—unhappily for all of them—easily ignored.

Their separation, a little over two years later, devastated her father. She'd let him down, she knew, but the stony finality of Luke leaving in the way he had that night meant she'd always known there could never be any apologies or reconciliations or returning to the past.

Her father's disappointment about her marriage and his pointed and pained resignation to life without grandchildren still made her feel terrible every time the subject was raised, but with time she'd grown a little more sanguine. She knew now that she had to live her life the way that was best for her and that was what she was trying to do.

She had no photographs of Luke in the house. Between him leaving and the week following the divorce she'd cleaned them out at the same time as she'd organised to have the interior completely redecorated. She hadn't wanted to give up her home but the reminders of him and of what they'd once had had been too painful for her to cope with. She'd destroyed most of her photos but the few she'd kept, along with her wedding album, were in boxes in storage in her father's attic. If she'd remembered before now Luke's connection to the picture he was holding, that would have gone there with the rest of them.

'I thought I was hallucinating when I saw this address on your file this afternoon,' Luke said slowly, almost absently, as if his attention was divided between the photograph and her in person. 'As far as I knew, you sold this place years ago. How did your father feel about paying out the money to me?'

'I've never told Daddy anything about our agreement over the house or the money,' Annabel told him quietly. She understood why he might think that was what she'd done, but she hadn't.

Luke had paid off the original loan on the house a few months prior to their separation and the property settlement negotiated between their solicitors had involved her paying a percentage of the value of the house back to him. He was right that her father would have given her the money if she'd asked—her mother had died before Annabel was old enough to remember her properly and until the advent of Luke she and her father had been very close—but by the time she'd had to come up with the sum itself it had felt important to her to do that on her own. 'My solicitor helped me arrange another mortgage so I could make the payment.'

Luke's brows rose fractionally as if her revelation surprised him. 'You didn't have to go that far. It never occurred to me you'd want to keep this place. If you'd told me we could have come to some arrangement about the money.'

'I didn't have a problem with the way we did it.' She shifted her bare feet and curled her toes into the thick beige carpet. She didn't like him being here. He was too big and too painfully familiar in her home. Changing the carpets and curtains and furniture and wallpaper, it hadn't altogether erased the memories of the deliriously happy first six months of their marriage. Seeing him standing in this room now made her chest hurt.

She was glad he'd come because it had felt important for her to voice her apology for hitting him, but now she'd done that she wanted him to go. She met his regard unblinkingly, hoping he'd take the hint. 'At the time it seemed important to have all debts between us settled as quickly as possible.'

He lifted his head, his eyes narrowing fractionally. 'Something's burning.'

'Oh, my soup!' Annabel whirled around and raced out to the kitchen, switched off the gas, plunged the smoking pan into the sink and filled it with water. The remains of the tomato liquid had thickened to a caramel-like syrup pool in the bottom and the rest of the pan was burnt and blackened. 'I can't believe I forgot,' she choked, struggling with the sash window above the taps to let out the smoke. 'I was about to eat but then I took a bath instead.'

She jumped out of the way as Luke came forward and wordlessly reached over her and jerked up the window. 'What if it'd caught fire?' he demanded. 'If you'd gone straight to bed you could have been killed.' He sent a scathing look towards the open cover of the smoke alarm he'd installed years earlier above the door. 'Why is that disabled?'

'It always goes off when I'm doing bacon so I took the battery out,' Annabel admitted guiltily. She registered the stone-cold sogginess of the toast she'd made earlier and grimaced. 'The one upstairs still works, I think.'

'You *think*?' Luke looked disgusted. He stalked past her towards the door. 'You're supposed to test it regularly.'

She hurried after him up the stairs. 'Luke, you can't just march about as if you still live here—'

'The battery's flat,' he interrupted, turning to scowl at her, tall enough to reach the tester button effortlessly without need of the chair she had to use.

'It was working a few months ago,' she protested defensively. 'It kept letting out beeps.'

'As it does when the battery's low,' he told her gratingly. 'How could you be so irresponsible? Have you checked this at all in the past six years?'

'Once or twice,' she said self-consciously.

'It's supposed to be done six-monthly.'

'I'll remember in future.'

'I can't believe Clancy hasn't—'

'Leave Geoffrey out of this. Don't you dare say anything to him.' She wouldn't put it past him to try, and the embarrassment of Luke haranguing poor Geoffrey about domestic responsibilities the other man knew nothing about didn't bear thinking about. 'He doesn't have anything to do with this.'

'Then it's time he realised—'

'It's not time for anything,' she cried over him. 'It really is nothing to do with Geoffrey, Luke. He's never even been here.'

'What?' Luke tilted his head, his expression instantly alert. 'What's going on, Annie?'

'Annabel,' she protested weakly. 'What you overheard yesterday in Outpatients was just Geoffrey being silly. We're not lovers. There's never been another man here. I prefer to live alone.'

'You deliberately let me think you were involved.'

'It felt as if you were prying.' She lifted her shoulders in an uncertain gesture. 'I resented it.'

For a few taut seconds their gazes held, his unreadable, Annabel's, she knew, nervous, then Luke closed his eyes briefly. 'I didn't come here to argue with you.'

She let her breath out slowly. 'Well, that's novel at least.'

His mouth tightened but he let the remark pass. 'What have you done in here?'

The door to the bedroom they'd once shared was ajar and before she could stop him Luke pushed it the rest of the way. He stopped in the doorway and inspected the room wordlessly.

'I just changed the wallpaper and curtains and I bought a new suite and wardrobe,' she said stiltedly, minimising the alterations a little because the reality was that she'd sold or given away everything he'd have been familiar with.

The paper, cream with a cool, delicate floral print, was a distinctly feminine design and she'd chosen it deliberately. This was her room now, the room where it was most important for there to be no reminder of the time she'd shared it with Luke. The Roman blinds bore a similar pale print and she'd replaced the solid antique furniture they'd both loved with a lighter, inexpensive, cream pine collection with brass fittings and ceramic floral decorations.

'Bit extreme, isn't it?' She felt his eyes on her face but kept her gaze firmly averted. 'Was it that important to wipe every trace of me away? You wouldn't know it for the same room.'

'I decided I preferred the bed by the window,' she told him shakily. 'And the wardrobe always looked a bit cramped over in that corner. I don't think the changes are extreme at all. I think they're a big improvement. I expect you don't like it because it seems too feminine now. But it suits me. Would you like some tea before you leave?' She wanted him gone now but she especially wanted him away from this room and, knowing him, she knew she'd achieve more by trying for that gently.

'I haven't done what I came for and that was to apologise properly to you for what happened this morning.' He spoke quietly, musingly, as if to himself, except his gaze, hard on her tight, flushing face, was directed entirely now at her. 'I had no right touching you the way I did but...I wasn't ready for how turned on I could still be by you, Annie. I thought I was over that a long time ago. What happened this morning, what I...wanted, was as much of a shock to me as it must have been for you.'

Annabel could hear the pulse of her blood throbbing thickly through her ears. She swallowed heavily. 'There was a time when we were very close,' she said huskily. 'It's not surprising we're both having a little trouble adjusting to our new situation.'

Unable to sustain the intensity of his gaze, she dropped her head. She knew he knew he hadn't been the only one who'd been aroused by the way he'd touched her, but that didn't mean she had the poise to cope with openly acknowledging it in front of him. Her recognition of her own *appalling* excitement was part of the reason she'd reacted so angrily to him.

Her sex drive had disappeared right along with Luke. In six years there'd been no other men, no thoughts even of other men, no fantasies and no arousal. She'd read somewhere that not just men but women, too, if they were deprived of sexual pleasure long enough, developed vividly erotic dream lives, but it wasn't true. Since the end of her marriage her dreams had never been anything other than unremarkable and chaste. She avoided sex on television, and in books and magazines it bored her and sent her page-flicking.

She'd felt nothing for years. Nothing. Not one, remote, tiny flicker of interest. Until Monday night, when she'd walked into Harry's drinks party and one look at Luke had set her paralysed senses reeling.

'I know I've said this before,' Annabel ventured huskily, 'but I still think the best thing we can do is put today behind us and start again afresh tomorrow.'

'Coward,' he said flatly. But to her relief he shifted away from her and moved towards the stairs. 'You used to have courage, Annie. You used to be strong and forthright and brave. When did you lose that?'

'The night you left me.'

The tightening of his face as he opened her front door told her that her barb had hit home, but it had simply been another lie, she registered wearily, despising herself for needing to hurt him like that. But telling the truth would have meant telling him she'd been brave until he'd touched her that morning. Telling the whole truth would have meant telling him her courage had lasted until his touch had forced her to acknowledge to herself how much she still wanted him.

And giving her ex-husband that sort of information, Annabel decided sickly, would have been nothing short of dangerous.

CHAPTER SIX

HANNAH called in sick with a cold on Monday morning so that Annabel's ward round took longer than usual. Then one of her surgical colleagues bleeped her to ask for urgent advice on a patient on one of the surgical wards. By the time she'd assessed him and arranged a change in his medication she was twenty minutes late for her morning clinic.

'There're a dozen waiting already,' Wendy, the nurse supervising her clinic, warned with a distracted smile when she brought in yet another set of notes to add to the thick pile on the bench in Annabel's examining room.

'I'm sorry, Annabel, but, looking at this lot, you're going to be here till after dark. You know they're cracking down on all the consultants' numbers at the moment. There've been arguments upstairs about how much nursing overtime has been costing these past two quarters down here. Geoffrey Clancy's already had Professor Geddes warning him this week that he has to finish on time from now on. If you don't watch out you'll be the next one called up to the big office.'

'I'm looking forward to it already.' Annabel's hands had curled into tight fists at the mention of her ex-husband and she forced herself to uncurl them again. She hadn't seen Luke since Wednesday night but how *typically* him, she thought savagely. A week in the job and he was already throwing orders around. If he tried sending one her way he'd be in for a shock.

'We're only seeing people who need to be seen and most of our clinic waiting lists are far too long already,' she muttered sourly. 'They need to allocate more money, not less care. We're not running a supermarket. What do they want us to do? Spend ten seconds with patients who've often waited months to see us then chuck them out the door?'

'I believe the official preferred time is five seconds,' Wendy said briskly, rolling her eyes as she bustled towards the door. 'But I'm glad to hear you complaining at last. You mustn't be a mouse, Annabel. If we all make a fuss maybe we'll get a bit of sense out of them upstairs. We need more staff, not patient cuts. I've put your Mrs Di Bella in room one and Mr Hill in three. Will your SHO be down to help, or are you on your own today?'

'Mark will come down if he can get away from the wards,' replied Annabel absently, studying her first patient's ECG tracing from that morning with a frown. Normally she began the clinic with follow-up appointments, before getting into new referrals, but she didn't remember this cardiogram. And this was clearly not going to be a five second consultation. 'Have I seen Mrs Di Bella before?'

'She's new.' Wendy opened the door. 'I put her first because the poor thing was so nervous she turned up an hour and a half early. The letter from her GP is just inside the notes.'

Annabel scanned the letter, before going into the next room. It seemed her patient was a forty-five-year-old woman who'd presented to the other doctor two weeks earlier with a history of breathlessness and intermittent heart palpitations.

'They're not there all the time, Doctor,' Mrs Di Bella told her once introductions were over and Annabel had begun to probe into her symptoms. 'Hardly at all sometimes.' She waved her arms about in a dismissive way, but beneath her superficial ebullience Annabel could see her face was pale and her expression strained.

'I've been rushing too much. My eldest daughter's getting married in six weeks and there are relatives coming to stay from all over the world and I've been crazy busy. She doesn't understand, you see, how much there is to do. You know these young girls, they think it's just a white dress and some pretty flowers. They don't understand how much there is to arrange.

'I'm a widow, Dr Stuart. My husband was killed in a car accident by a drunk driver two years ago so there's only me to do all the organising. I can't be sick. There's no time for me to be sick. Please, tell me there's nothing to worry about.'

'Tell me more about your breathlessness,' Annabel instructed. 'You say it's mostly when you lean forward?'

'Or bending over, sometimes if I'm sitting,' the older woman agreed. 'It goes away if I lie flat.'

Annabel wondered about that. In most types of heart disease breathlessness was caused by the accumulation of fluid in the lungs and was made worse by lying down. She finished taking a history and then examined her patient carefully. 'What are these?' she asked, frowning at the small red lesions on her patient's fingers and palms as she inspected the trembling hands. 'How long have you had these?'

'A few weeks.' Mrs Di Bella shrugged but her eyes were worried. 'Perhaps months. They're little sores, I thought. They're a little painful, but they go away on their own in a few days or a week or so. They're nothing, are they, Doctor?'

Annabel checked her feet, noting similar lesions there, too. 'Do you ever have dizzy spells?' she asked, examining the rest of Mrs Di Bella's skin and inside her mouth and her eyes. 'Funny turns, fainting, pins and needles attacks, anything like that?'

'Just the heart thumping.'

'No hot flushes? Sweating in the night?'

'I do get hot sometimes. Occasionally I have to get up to change the sheets. I put that down to going through the change, Doctor.'

'Are you still having periods?'

'Just every few months,' Mrs Di Bella revealed. 'Not regular, the way I used to be. Is that what it is, Dr Stuart? Do you think it's the change of life?'

Annabel wished she could reassure her on that but she couldn't. 'Have you lost weight at all, Mrs Di Bella?'

'Quite a bit.' Her patient's pallor deepened. 'About fifteen pounds. But with all the preparations for the wedding...' She trailed off, wringing her hands together. 'My doctor says my blood pressure is very good.'

'It is,' Annabel agreed, checking the note of it one of the clinic nurses had made earlier. 'It's perfect.' She took out her stethoscope and sat Mrs Di Bella forward to listen to her chest properly. 'Breathe out normally,' she said quietly when her patient held her breath. 'At the moment I'm just listening to your heart.'

'He said my blood tests were good, too,' Mrs Di Bella told her anxiously when she'd finished that part of her examination.

'All the results I've looked at appear completely normal,' Annabel confirmed. The GP had had copies forwarded to her and she'd checked them when she'd read his letter.

Finally, she used an ophthalmoscope, a small portable, torch-like device with lenses for examining the inside of the eye, to look for lesions of a similar nature to the ones on Mrs Di Bella's hands and feet, but thankfully her eyes were clear.

When she was finished, she lowered the back of the bed again so Mrs Di Bella could lean back. 'This jelly will just feel a little cold on your chest,' she warned, explaining what she was doing as she squeezed clear lubricating jelly from a tube across the front of her patient's chest, then picked up the probe of her ECHO machine. 'This machine's called an echocardiograph,' she explained. 'It shows me pictures of your heart. I promise it won't hurt.'

Annabel moved the probe across Mrs Di Bella's chest slowly, first getting a general picture on her screen of the way her patient's heart was functioning and then narrowing in on the area she was concerned about.

When she'd finished she wiped away the jelly with tissues, helped her patient back into her gown and sat on the edge of the bed. 'Is there anyone waiting for you in the waiting room, Mrs Di Bella? Is your daughter with you today, or have you brought a friend?'

The older woman shook her head vigorously. 'I came alone, Dr Stuart. Is it serious? If you've something to say, please, just tell me. I have to know. Please. I have so much to organise. What do you think?'

Ideally Annabel liked to have someone with patients when she had bad news but obviously in this case circumstances weren't ideal and she was sure that delaying what she wanted to say would merely increase Mrs Di Bella's already considerable anxiety. 'The ECG the technician took when you arrived here this morning shows that your heart rhythm is abnormal,' Annabel said gently. 'It's in a rhythm we call atrial fibrillation. What that means is that there's some disruption to the electrical system in your heart.'

Her patient crossed herself. 'This is serious?' she whispered.

'Atrial fibrillation in itself can be caused by dozens of things,' Annabel explained. 'Sometimes we never discover what's causing it and some people can have this sort of rhythm for years without us knowing about it. But in your case I know the reason because on the scan I just did I can see a lump on one of your heart walls between the top parts of your heart.'

She drew a picture on the back of her notes, outlining the anatomy of the heart. 'Here, you see,' she said quietly, drawing the large mass she'd seen. 'There's a type of tumour growing here and it's upsetting your heart rhythm. It's causing your breathing problems and I suspect the bumps on your skin are because blood clots forming on the lump here are being thrown off occasionally and then they're getting stuck in the tiny blood vessels in your hands and feet.'

'Oh, Doctor.' Mrs Di Bella clutched at Annabel's hands. 'How long do I have?'

'It's not fatal.' Annabel squeezed the older woman's trembling hands reassuringly. 'Or, at least, only very rarely. This is a rare sort of tumour which usually behaves completely benignly. The treatment involves admitting you today to give you some blood-thinning medication to stop any more blood clots forming, then surgery as soon as possible to remove the tumour and repair the hole where it's been. You're going to need an operation, Mrs Di Bella. Soon. If all goes well there's no reason to think you'll lead anything but a normal life. Now, with your permission I'd like to speak with one of our surgeons today.'

'Is it a big operation?'

'All heart surgery is big,' Annabel admitted.

'But the wedding…?'

'You'll be there. After your operation. But I don't want you worrying about weddings in the meantime. Your daughter and her fiancé and his family are going to have

to take over the organising for you. You're going to have
to delegate.'

'I'll write lists.' Her patient slumped back against the
bed, her eyes wide. 'Long, long lists. But, God willing, I
will be at the wedding?'

'God willing,' Annabel confirmed.

'I did know it was serious,' the other woman whispered.
'I don't know how but I just knew it was serious.'

'That's often the way,' Annabel said gently. 'Pop your
clothes on, Mrs Di Bella. I'll go and telephone the surgeon
and see where he would like me to send you. I'll be back
in a few minutes.'

Happily Simon Rawlings was holding a clinic in
Outpatients as well and once Annabel had explained Mrs
Di Bella's case he agreed to see her immediately. 'Send
her straight across, Annabel,' he told her heartily. 'I'll
squeeze her in now.'

Annabel offered to try and get better ECHO pictures by
sedating Mrs Di Bella and passing a lead down into her
oesophagus, but he told her not to worry about that.

'We'll organise to get good pictures tomorrow with an
MRI scan,' he told her confidently, referring to another type
of scan particularly useful for outlining the anatomy of the
heart. 'We've space on our surgical list for Thursday if we
can get her worked up in time. Is she otherwise well?'

'She gets a rash with sulphur antibiotics but no other
problems,' Annabel confirmed. 'Thanks, Simon.'

'No problem. Young Tamsin Winston's doing well. Have
you seen her yet today?'

'I was running late this morning,' Annabel admitted.
'I'm planning on visiting this afternoon.'

'She had breakfast today and she'll be leaving the unit
after lunch,' the surgeon told her. 'You did a good job,
assessing her so quickly and getting her to us.'

'Thank Luke for that,' Annabel told him. 'I was just the onlooker.'

'He seems a capable sort of chap,' Simon said stoutly. 'I was impressed with him yesterday. I hear he's stirred up the trust about the delay in approving the medical budget next year. There's been a rumour he got it all rubber-stamped over the weekend.'

'That's the first I've heard of it.' Annabel's teeth gritted at this, the second source of confirmation that Luke was indeed making waves, but then she realised that on the particular issue of funding he had her support. In his po-sition she might have been more diplomatic in her approach to the trust, but it wasn't in Luke's nature to twiddle his thumbs patiently while the board prevaricated. And clearly his intervention had been good for the department. Harry had been tiptoeing around nervously about the department's funding for months and getting nowhere.

Wendy put her head around the door as Annabel was finishing her call. 'Annabel, we're getting way behind.'

'Sorry.' Annabel hurriedly wrote in Mrs Di Bella's notes. 'I couldn't rush this one. Mrs Di Bella has to go straight across to Simon Rawlings's clinic. He's going to admit her under his care. Can you spare a nurse to go with her, Wendy? She's had a bit of a shock.'

'Bad news?'

'Looks like an atrial myxoma,' Annabel confirmed. 'Simon's going to try and fit her in for surgery on Thursday.'

'I'll take her myself.' Wendy took the notes and passed Annabel a new set. 'Mr Hill's in three. He'll only take a few minutes. I've put your next one in two and Professor Geddes is next door in five, seeing some of your new gen-eral referrals.'

Annabel looked up sharply. *'What?'*

'He happened to be going by and he was a bit concerned about how many people were waiting. When I explained about Hannah being sick today and you being on your own he decided to help,' Wendy said calmly. 'He's ever so nice, isn't he? I expect he needs to build up his own list as well. You don't mind, do you, Annabel?'

'Mind? Why would I mind?' Just because the man who was effectively now her boss had decided she was too slow to be able to manage her clinic in the efficient way he clearly demanded, what reason in the world would she have for minding? Annabel picked up a set of notes at random. 'Mr Hill's in four, you said.'

Wendy sent her a strange look. 'Three,' she said slowly. 'Mr Hill's in room three. The Professor's in four.'

Although he shared her clinic, Luke clearly didn't feel any need to consult with her about any of the cases he saw because she didn't see anything of him until the next afternoon when he turned up late to chair the medical department's monthly meeting in one of the seminar rooms on the top floor of the hospital.

'Harry won't be with us today,' he announced with an easy air of command and a confident nod to Annabel, along with all the other gathered physicians who'd just spent almost twenty minutes of precious time waiting for him to show up.

If she'd been braver, Annabel speculated from the safety of her carefully chosen chair as far away from Luke as it was possible to sit, she might have voiced some protest about his tardiness. But the plain fact was that where Luke was concerned she'd decided that avoidance was the only way she was going to be able to cope with him. Besides, as she already knew, her courage was non-existent. The last vestiges of it had flown out the window, along with her self-respect and peace of mind, that morning in the X-ray changing room.

And if she didn't protest about Luke being late, no one else would. She looked around her colleagues with a resigned expression. Out of the twenty or so gathered doctors in the room she was the only one not sitting at full attention, eager to hear the great man speak.

'He's taken an extra couple of days on the weekend for his fishing trip,' Luke added evenly. 'Sorry I've kept you waiting.' But he offered no excuse, merely swung himself around into the leather chair at the head of the table, checked his watch as if he was in a hurry, then directed one of his particularly charming brand of smiles towards Harry's secretary. 'Mary, minutes from the last meeting, please.'

'I've got them right here, Professor Geddes.'

Annabel, noting the secretary's flush and tremulous smile as she scrambled to collect her notes, felt ill. Mary might be fifty-five and proud grandmother of seven, but she was a woman and it seemed that meant she was as susceptible to Luke's appeal as the rest of them were.

After dispensing with the minutes, Luke went on to deal rapidly with each item on the formal printed agenda they'd all unexpectedly found in their pigeon-holes the previous afternoon. Although his brisk efficiency and the consequent lack of discussion, let alone dissent, seemed to be adding to his already astronomical approval rating among her colleagues, Annabel felt a sad wave of nostalgia for the passing of Harry's more rambling, democratic, if bureaucratic style of leadership.

'That has to be a world record,' murmured Geoffrey beside her as the meeting drew rapidly to a close. He shook his watch, as if doubting its accuracy. 'Twenty minutes. We used to be here two hours with Harry.'

Annabel pointed out he was forgetting the extra twenty minutes Luke had kept them waiting, but Geoffrey merely shrugged. 'We still come out way ahead,' he said cheerfully. The group was dispersing and they joined the throng moving towards the door. 'It's a long time since we've got away this early,' Geoffrey remarked. 'Feel like catching a film tonight?'

Annabel blinked. 'On a Tuesday?'

'Why not?'

She stopped, hesitating, allowing the other doctors to move around them out of the room. She had spent the occasional pleasant Saturday evening—once every three or four months or so—seeing a movie or play with Geoffrey, but she supposed there wasn't any reason why they couldn't go to a film during the week. She had paperwork to catch up on but suddenly the idea of being able to lose herself in a movie for a couple of hours appealed to her. 'What's on?'

'There's a new comedy at Whitley's. It's tipped for awards and it's had good reviews. It starts at eight-forty.'

'OK.' Annabel nodded abruptly. 'Why not? I'll meet you there ten minutes before. If you get there before me, go ahead and buy the tickets and I'll settle up with you when I arrive.'

That earned her a mysteriously impatient look but he merely said, 'I'll book to be sure. Make it seven-thirty and we'll grab a snack.'

'Fine.' That at least would save her having to cook. 'Seven-thirty.'

'Great.' Geoffrey grinned and looked as if he was about to add something more but Luke's voice cut in on them.

'Sorry to interrupt, Geoffrey, but I need Annabel for a few seconds.'

'No problem. We're finished.' Although Annabel froze

immediately, Geoffrey seemed to find Luke's request unremarkable and he merely nodded and moved out after the
last of their colleagues. 'See you tonight, Annabel.'

'Seven-thirty,' Annabel repeated automatically. She
waited until he'd left then turned to Luke, feeling herself
flush as she met his cool look and realised he'd overheard
every word of her conversation with Geoffrey. 'Is this important?' she asked crisply. 'I was just about to leave.'

'Your bleeper's not working,' he said smoothly.

She faltered. 'What?'

'Your bleeper.' With an easy movement he lifted her
bleeper out of the breast pocket of her white coat and
pressed the test button, demonstrating its lack of response.
'Do you have a mental block about replacing all batteries?'

'It was fine this morning.' Annabel's skin had shivered
at the brief brush of his fingers when he'd removed her
bleeper and, ignoring his taunt, she took a hasty step back.
She'd been bleeped several times during her clinic but now
she thought about it she realised it had been quiet most of
the afternoon. She took the device back from him and tested
it, confirming for herself that he'd been right about the
batteries. 'I'll take it to Switchboard. Thank you for letting
me know. How did you find out it wasn't working?'

'A GP was trying to get hold of you. When he gave up
half an hour ago Switchboard put him though to me as I
was on call. He wants us to admit one of your patients,
Daisy Miller.'

'Daisy?' Annabel lifted her head sharply. 'Did you tell
him to send her in? Is she in failure?'

'She's coming in and it sounds like it,' he confirmed.

'I only discharged her last week,' Annabel said slowly.
She chewed at her lower lip. 'She's supposed to be coming
to clinic on Friday.' The frequency of Daisy's admissions
worried her enormously. It was looking as if they had far

less time than they'd hoped to wait for her transplant. 'I'll have a look at her. Did you tell him to send her to M ward?'

'M's full but there's a bed on J so she's going there.' Luke's bleeper shrilled at that moment and he checked the number and went back to the telephone at the desk. 'I imagine that'll be her now,' he told her. 'Let me check.'

His conversation was brief and to the point and Annabel could tell before he'd finished that it was about Daisy and that she was very sick. She left him and started running for the ward.

Luke caught up with her before she got to the stairs. 'I'm on call, Annie.' She was puffing but he wasn't even out of breath. 'You have plans. I'll look after her. Go home.'

'No, I want to see her.' She wasn't worrying about missing the movie. Geoffrey always carried his mobile so she'd be able to get hold of him and let him know in advance if Daisy proved too unwell to leave.

Nurses were hurrying about, fitting monitors and a blood-pressure cuff and drawing up drugs, and the on-call registrar was already with Daisy when they got to the ward. He was trying to put a line into one of the veins in her arm, but didn't seem to be having any luck finding one. He stepped aside quickly when Luke motioned that he'd take over.

Annabel, paling, went forward quickly and took Daisy's cold hand, murmuring words of comfort while she examined her. She'd thought Daisy had been bad on her last admission but she was far worse now. Behind her oxygen mask she was gasping desperately for breath, her blood pressure was ominously low and her skin was thick-looking, doughy and blue-tinged.

Her liver was huge as well, no doubt swollen with fluid. Annabel did her best to manage a reassuring smile when Daisy sent her a grateful grimace between heaving breaths.

'It'll just be a few minutes,' she told her patient. 'We'll get this line in and get the drugs in and you'll start feeling better immediately.' She let go Daisy's hand so she could hold the stethoscope to the young woman's heart and lungs, checking the heart sounds and confirming the severity of her heart failure by the crackles of fluid that could be heard bubbling in her lungs.

Luke had already slid a line smoothly into place and Annabel looked at the nurse holding the diuretic he'd requested. 'Better start with one-twenty,' she said quietly, amending the dose he'd ordered. 'She's on maintenance eighty milligrams as it is. Her blood pressure's up just enough to handle it.'

'Ten of morphine,' Luke ordered, along with an antiemetic to prevent any nausea, nodding acknowledgement of Annabel's suggestion as he gave a second syringe of the diuretic then held Daisy's arm high in the air and massaged it to speed up the movement of the drugs into her heart. He reached for an ampoule of a drug that would dilate Daisy's blood vessels and help prevent kidney damage and gave it to one of the nurses with instructions on how he wanted it diluted. 'Someone get X-Ray up here stat.'

It took them a very long forty minutes to get Daisy marginally stabilised, but by the time Annabel returned with the ward's portable ECHO machine less than ten minutes later the fascinated way her young patient was gazing up at Luke, busy adjusting one of her infusion rates, told her Daisy was now improving fast. This time at least.

Daisy tore her eyes away from Luke long enough to send a solemn look in Annabel's direction. 'Wow!' she mouthed.

Annabel rolled her eyes. 'Daisy, this is Professor Geddes,' she said evenly, trying not to appear too cynical. 'He's recently joined us here on staff at St Peter's.'

'Oh, I've heard of you,' Daisy gasped, between breaths.

'You're famous. I've read some of the stuff you've written on the net. You're the same as Dr Stuart.' She fluttered her lashes. 'You specialise in heart conditions like mine, don't you?'

'That's right.' Luke turned on a smile that would have made Annabel's heart flip if it had been directed at her and which made her heart tremble anyway even though it wasn't. 'Annabel and I share a similar interest in the field. Tell me, Daisy, what do you think of your cardiac trace now?'

Daisy tore her gaze away from him, tipped her head back and eyed her rhythm dispassionately. 'Don't freak out,' she told him breathlessly. 'That's normal for me. I always throw off dozens of those extra beats, don't I, Dr Stuart?'

'You do,' Annabel confirmed, watching the trace, too. She knew why Luke had asked. He wasn't just testing Daisy's knowledge of her disease. While she had been in acute failure the frequency of extra heart beats had been much higher. He'd been worried about her going into VT then V Fib, potentially fatal disordered heart rhythms. 'Daisy's never had rhythm problems,' she told him quietly. 'At least none we're aware of.'

'Touch wood.' Daisy banged her knuckles on the board behind her head.

While Annabel was setting up to check Daisy's heart with her ECHO machine, Luke left them, murmuring he'd be back in a few minutes after he'd called Daisy's GP and let him know what was happening.

'Is he married?' Daisy whispered, as soon as they were alone.

'He's too old for you and I thought you were going out with a footballer,' Annabel murmured distractedly as she adjusted the settings on her machine.

'I love John but if I thought a guy like Professor Geddes

would look at me twice I might have second thoughts,'
Daisy told her between breaths. 'Do you think he likes me?'

'Of course.' Annabel smeared jelly across her young patient's chest. 'Everyone likes you.'

'Pity I'm too sick to do anything about it.' Daisy pouted
and sagged back against the bed. '*You* could, though, Dr
Stuart. Do *you* fancy him?'

Annabel rolled her eyes. 'I suppose you've been racing
about like a madwoman this past week,' she mused, moving
her probe to get a better picture of Daisy's left ventricle. 'I
should have kept you in hospital. All-night raves and champagne breakfasts at the Ritz, I expect.'

'I wish.' Daisy gave a wheezy giggle. 'No, John's quite
boring, really. We went out one night to a club but we
weren't late.' She paused to catch her breath again. 'He has
to be in bed early, you know, most nights. And he's not
supposed to drink. It's in his contract. They're very strict.'

'Your ejection fraction's down.' Annabel frowned as she
checked the figure calculated by the computer in her machine from measurements she took, comparing the size of
her patient's heart before and after a contraction. She felt
the hairs on the back of her neck prickle and knew Luke
must have come back into the room so she went through
the scan again for him to watch. 'Definite changes from a
week ago,' she told him.

'I'll have a look at the old figures.' He came around to
the other side of the bed and checked Daisy's infusion.
'Don't delay your plans for the evening, Annabel. You
should have been off duty more than an hour ago. You can
leave Daisy to me now. You don't mind, do you, Daisy?'

'Oh, no,' Daisy said huskily, and Annabel registered with
resigned irritation the rapt attention with which the younger
woman was gazing up at Luke again. 'I'm fine. Don't
worry about me, Dr Stuart.'

Annabel resented him involving Daisy in their discussion. 'I thought I'd stay another hour or so,' she said stiffly. 'Just to make sure—'

'Go,' Luke interrupted calmly.

Ignoring Daisy's intrigued expression, Annabel tissued the gel from her chest, disconnected the ECHO machine and moved it away from the bed. She directed a meaningful glare towards Luke then walked carefully towards the door. 'I'm just going to make a phone call at the desk,' she announced coolly. 'I'll be back in a few minutes.'

But Luke got to her before she'd even finished dialling Geoffrey's mobile number. Reaching over her, he disconnected the phone and took the receiver out of her hand.

'What are you doing?' Annabel turned around slowly to confront him, her eyes flashing even if she had to keep her tone low lest the nurses doing their six o'clock drug round in the cubical opposite overheard them. 'For heaven's sake—'

'You're being childish,' he said softly. 'You're fighting me on principle, Annabel, not because there's any need. I'm perfectly capable of handling—'

'I know that,' she interrupted. 'Of course I know that.' She might have had a special interest in Daisy's disease but Luke was a world authority on it. His experience vastly exceeded hers. 'However, she happens to be my patient.'

'You're not on call tonight.'

'I feel I should stay another hour or so to be sure she's stable.'

'You're leaving.' His hands on her shoulders, he steered her with—for him—surprising gentleness, away from the desk and along the ward. 'You're running out of time for your date.'

'It isn't a date,' she protested. 'Why do you keep going

on like this? It's just friends, going to a movie. Geoffrey won't care if I cancel—'

With an air of weary impatience Luke pushed her into one of the doctors' offices, turned on the light, then closed the door behind them. 'Annabel, in the past six years how many lovers have you had?'

CHAPTER SEVEN

How many lovers had she had? Annabel felt sick. 'That's none of your business,' she gasped eventually.

'Ten?' Luke waited a fraction of a second and when she didn't respond he added less tolerantly, 'Five? Two? *One?*'

She opened her mouth then closed it again, paralysed with shock.

'None.' He sighed. He inspected her heavy white coat, the generously cut jacket and full skirt and tights she wore, his regard brutally unflattering. 'What's wrong with you, Annabel? What's happened to the girl I married? What happened to that laughing, sexy girl from that photograph I picked up last week?'

'She was ludicrous,' Annabel said stonily. 'You know that as well as I do. She was young and stupid and sad and pathetic.'

'You left out ten times the woman you are now,' he countered flatly. 'She was warm and spirited and energetic, bursting with life and intensely, lovingly, joyfully sexual.'

'And look what that got her,' Annabel flung at him. 'You! Some good that did either of us!'

'Don't even begin to go there,' Luke warned softly, dangerous sparks flaring in the green depths of his eyes. 'Don't even think about starting on that, Annabel, because we'll be here all night, working through that.'

'I want to get out,' she cried.

'When I've finished.' He leaned back against the door. He looked big and determined and he was obviously not going anywhere. Annabel knew she'd get exactly nowhere if she tried pushing him. 'Before I knew you were working here at St Peter's I meant to look you up when I arrived in London.'

His words surprised her but she kept her expression blank. 'So?'

'So I expected to find you all grown up, contentedly remarried and probably nursing a couple of babies by now.'

'*Babies?*' Annabel sucked in her breath. '*What?*'

'You looked good holding Tamsin Winston's baby. And you always wanted children.'

'Yes, years ago,' she agreed faintly. She expected most women in love experienced the desire to bear their lover's child. But it was a long time since she'd let herself remember she'd also had those sort of desires. 'But children need two parents.'

'So why aren't you married?'

'I haven't met anyone.'

'Why do you think that is?'

'That's a ludicrous question,' she protested. 'There's no answer. I just haven't.'

'The reason you haven't, Annie,' he said calmly, 'is that in six years you've turned yourself from an exciting, passionate, *living* woman into a repressed, uptight, frustrated zombie with an army haircut and the wardrobe of a woman thirty years your senior.'

His eyes calmly registered the trembling hand she lifted to her cropped hair. 'You've destroyed the house,' he continued gently, his observations rendered somehow more painful for having been delivered in the warmly reasonable, almost kindly tone he'd adopted. 'You've turned a warm, welcoming home into some horror out of a decorating catalogue, and if you hitting me then letting soup boil dry last week are signs that what happened between us that day shook you up a bit I'm glad, because the one thing you need right now is shaking up.'

She glared at him with hate in her eyes. 'Go to hell.'

'Been there,' he said roughly. 'And I wasn't offering to do any more shaking, Annie, because I doubt my sanity could take it. But what you're going to do is put a smile on your face and some lipstick on that argumentative mouth of yours. You're going to meet Clancy tonight and you're going to give him a chance while he's still willing and you've still got the body of a goddess to attract him. If another six years without sex does the same to you as the past six, he might just be your last chance.'

Annabel said something she'd never said before, something obscene and succinct and entirely to the point, but Luke's composure didn't falter for even a second. He merely stood aside from the door and opened it, allowing her to get out.

'Good to hear you're still capable of expressing a little honest emotion,' he remarked calmly. 'Keep it up. It's almost seven. You'll have to hurry to reach Clancy in time. Have fun.'

She sent him a savage look then stormed straight upstairs to her office. She slammed the door, locked it, dragged her spare white coat from the hook at the back of the door, threw it to the floor and stared unflinchingly into the small mirror the coat had been covering.

She was a dried-up old hag, she told herself faintly, wiping the hot tears which had formed after she'd fled Luke out of her eyes with the heels of her hands, forcing herself not to flinch away from her reflection. Essentially, that's what he'd said. She was a dried-up, frustrated, screwed-up hag, with hair like a soldier and matronly clothes.

But instead of seeing the grotesque, repugnant monster she was half expecting, she was a little startled to see that she looked—apart from her red, blotchy eyes and temper stains on her cheeks—the same as she always looked.

Her hair was short, yes, too short to be particularly flattering, but although it was a long time since she'd paid it any sort of specialised attention outside its two-monthly trim it was soft and shiny and still a vibrant, coppery red, with no signs yet of her colour fading. And the way it feathered around her forehead and ears wasn't at all army-like.

While her features might be unbalanced, her grey eyes too big and widely spaced in her small face for beauty, her skin was unlined and creamy and clear.

She shed her white doctor's coat and took a step back, peering with dry eyes now at the scarf tucked into the buttoned-top of her blouse and her padded-shouldered jacket. The scarf might be too much, she acknowledged, tugging at the silk until it slid free. And the jacket, while roomy and comfortable—the way she preferred them—added several unnecessarily puffy inches of bulk around her chest and shoulders.

She unbuttoned her jacket so that it hung loosely like a coat, rather than bunching around her, and that at least left the line of her figure unadorned and clean. It was only her clothes she'd changed these past years, she knew. Her figure and size hadn't altered especially. Her breasts, certainly, while still too big in her opinion, remained rounded and firm, from her skirt size she knew her waist hadn't shrunk or expanded particularly and for her height her legs were relatively long and well shaped.

Part of her rebelled against Luke's scathing criticism, but the other part, the fragile part, still wondered sickly if he could have been right. She turned sideways experimentally then came closer and peered at her face. What if he'd been right about her being ugly now and she was just so used to looking at herself she hadn't realised?

The doctor part of her might not care—in fact, hadn't cared for years—but was the woman inside her ready to resign herself to that yet? Until Luke had come back she had been, but now she'd realised that she was still capable of responding sexually to a man she wasn't sure how she felt any more. Was she really ready to face a future where she was destined to always remain alone and childless? She might never find a man she loved as much as Luke but perhaps, if she made more of herself, she might one day interest a man who could arouse milder yet still satisfying feelings in her.

She collected her discarded coat and scarf and, after draping them over the back of her chair, retrieved her handbag from her desk and marched back towards the door. She'd think about it when she was less upset, she decided. But the one thing she certainly wasn't going to do, she vowed silently, was to mope morosely about her office and stand up Geoffrey, giving Luke yet more reasons to ridicule her.

There wasn't time to go home first to change her clothes so she drove directly to the shopping centre, parked her little car, then dashed through and up the escalators to the area outside the cinemas where they'd arranged to meet. She saw Geoffrey a little while before she reached him. He was talking to a couple in the ticket queue. As she got closer she stopped, hesitating nervously, realising she knew the pair.

Geoffrey must have already collected his tickets because he was outside the barrier, but to her relief the queue suddenly moved quickly and the other two said their goodbyes, moved up to one of the counters, bought tickets, waved, then moved inside into the theatre complex.

Annabel walked slowly towards Geoffrey. She knew immediately from the stunned way he turned to look at her that they'd been talking about her. And Luke. 'Annabel—'

'I saw you,' she said faintly. 'And Abdul and Louise.' She hadn't seen either of the other doctors for several years but they'd once been medical registrars at the Free with Luke.

'We trained at Guy's together.' Geoffrey still looked incredulous. 'I used to play golf with Abdul. They know Luke. They'd heard he'd arrived at St Peter's and they were curious to know how you two were getting on.'

'I know what they must have told you.' Annabel winced. 'It's true. I'm sorry.'

'*Married*, Annabel.' He shook his head slowly at her. '*Married!* I can't believe it. Harry mentioned something the other day about the two of you knowing each other, but…I didn't know you'd ever been seriously involved with anyone before. Why on earth didn't you say anything?'

'It was a long time ago,' she said lamely. 'I didn't feel up to facing any gossip when he came back. It was years ago, Geoffrey. It's not like—' She broke off. 'Luke and I hadn't seen each other in six years. It didn't seem important.'

'That first day in Outpatients when he walked in on us I thought there was something strange going on. Was he angry about catching you with me?'

'*Angry?*' Annabel blinked. 'Oh, *jealous*, you mean?' She almost laughed out loud at his hesitant nod. 'Oh, no, Geoffrey. Oh, no, you mustn't think that. Don't worry. Considering what he thinks of me now, if he was anything it would have been astounded.'

'Can we?… Look…' He waved the tickets at her. 'This all seems to have thrown me a bit. I'm not that interested in the movie. Would you mind if we gave up on it?'

She shook her head. She felt so guilty about him finding out about Luke this way she'd have gone along with whatever he'd wanted. She stood quietly by while he gave the tickets away to a young couple near the back of the queue.

He guided her to a small Greek restaurant in Bayswater a little way from the cinema. They sat at one end of a long table and Geoffrey, who'd obviously been there before, exchanged greetings with the friendly woman who came to take their order. After checking with Annabel to see she had no objections, he turned down the offer of menus and left the choice of food up to the chef.

'Everything here's delicious,' he told Annabel quietly. 'I've been coming here for years and I've never been disappointed. Annabel, I'm not sure what to say. Do you want to talk about it or would you rather I didn't ask?'

'There's nothing really to say,' Annabel said warily. 'I was quite young, we married, it lasted two years, he left and went to Boston and the next year we were divorced. According to Harry, he's never remarried.' She felt her mouth tighten. 'I don't imagine he lacks for sex and as he's never seemed to have wanted children I suppose he doesn't feel the need.'

'Do you have feelings for him?'

'*Feelings?*' She grimaced. 'What a strange word that is. I'll always have some…feelings for Luke, Geoffrey, the divorce didn't change that. Those sorts of emotions don't just disappear when it's convenient. I don't know if you've ever been through this sort of thing yourself, but even after a gap of several years it's hard going straight into a normal social relationship. I don't think Luke's finding it easy either but…well, we're working on it.'

She sat back for the delivery of a basket of bread and a selection of dips and little entrées, thanked their waitress, then met Geoffrey's brown regard levelly. 'It's been a confusing few months. Until Harry told me Luke was coming to St Peter's the whole thing about me ever having been married had been irrelevant, and afterwards I was too worried to want to talk about it to anyone.'

To her relief, his smile was gently understanding. 'It doesn't matter,' he said quietly. 'It's none of my business anyway. Would you like bread?'

She had no appetite but he seemed eager for her to try the food and for his sake she took some of the warm, flat bread and spread it with pale taramasalata and a garlic-flavoured yoghurt dip in turn. Both were delicious and she felt a little of her hunger reviving as she accepted a small rice-filled vine leaf and found it refreshing, redolent with fresh mint and very tasty.

For a little while they ate quietly, then Geoffrey said, 'You're not thinking about leaving St Peter's, are you?'

'The thought has crossed my mind,' Annabel admitted. She took a mouthful of the lemon-scented water they'd been brought, and put her glass down with a sigh. 'I don't want to leave. I love the hospital. But I did find myself looking through the job adds in *The Lancet* this week rather thoroughly.'

'Was your divorce that acrimonious?'

'The divorce was a breeze.' She bit at her lower lip. 'The acrimonious bit was the marriage.' The details weren't something she'd ever considered discussing before but she was still stinging from her earlier encounter with Luke. 'Men like Luke want doormat wives, not women with minds and opinions of their own.'

Geoffrey blinked. 'Luke doesn't strike me as the sort of person who wouldn't want an equal partner,' he said slowly.

'You only think that because you haven't tried disagreeing with him yet,' she told him silkily.

He looked taken aback by that and Annabel felt herself flushing. 'I didn't mean it to come out like that,' she admitted sheepishly. 'The truth is, there were faults on both sides. If I'd been less blinded by infatuation in the beginning I'd have realised how incompatible we were before we married.'

'From what Abdul and Louise were saying, you must have only been a house officer the first year you were married, and they mentioned Luke was still a registrar.' Geoffrey looked over the white beans he was dishing up for them both. 'With those sorts of working hours you can't have been able to spend much time together. That wouldn't have been a good start for any marriage.'

'Those two years were pretty hellish hours-wise for both of us,' she admitted. 'Luke was on a demanding rotation then when he took a consultant job I went from two frantic house officer attachments to my first medical SHO year so I was just as busy. I was on one in three incredibly busy call all that time and on my nights off duty I'd often be so tired I'd fall asleep in my room at the hospital and not get home at all. But Luke was worse. He was devoted to his job. He made himself available to the hospital seven days a week, twenty-four hours a day. He'd go in weekends, nights, whenever he was needed, regardless of whether I'd made plans or if we hadn't seen each other in ages.

'The first six months we were married we still tried really hard to scrape time away for each other and we had quite a few weekend breaks abroad and even a week's holiday in Greece, but then Luke was offered a job in Boston and things started going wrong,' she confided tiredly. She contemplated the dish of tiny octopuses in front of her.

'He wanted to take the job, you see. He wanted me to come to America with him. He couldn't believe it when I refused. He just couldn't understand that I might not be prepared to leave my home and my job and my father and just race off overseas with him, all for the sake of him getting just that little bit further ahead on the career ladder. He'd been so sure I'd simply uproot myself and go happily wherever he wanted he'd even made enquiries about an internal medicine residency for me behind my back.

'We never really recovered from that. He resented me for holding up his career and I resented him for not loving me enough to think to put me first.'

'But obviously he did.' Geoffrey blinked at her. 'He stayed, didn't he?'

'Unwillingly,' she said quietly. 'Oh, he never said as much but it was obvious. He used to get letters from Harvard every six months so I knew he was keeping in touch and we always argued more around the time they came. And he certainly didn't waste any time flying straight over there after he left me. But the harm had been with that first job offer.

'After that I started feeling insecure about all sorts of things, including whether he really loved me or not and even about other women. I never realised how forceful my own sex could be until I saw how they came on to him all the time.' She lifted her head and smiled wryly. 'Even when I was with him they'd still smile and watch him and flirt. They used to make me feel invisible.'

She saw Geoffrey's wistful expression and grimaced. 'It wasn't fun, Geoffrey. At least not for me. I had to bite my hands to stop myself from screaming at them and it was like torture, imagining him with them, when I was stuck at work for days on end. I couldn't forget that I'd once been one of those women chasing him, and I'd got what I'd wanted so why wouldn't other women get the same thing?'

'Luke doesn't seem the type to take advantage of his looks,' Geoffrey contributed quietly.

'Well, that's the irony of it all,' Annabel admitted huskily. 'He's a very moral person. Integrity is important to him. I doubt he was ever physically unfaithful to me.' She sighed. 'Which is probably the reason he used to hate it so much when I didn't trust him.'

'So you drifted apart?'

'More burst apart, really.' She put down her fork. 'I started wanting a baby but he kept saying no. Subconsciously, I suspect I realised that that was because he'd already decided we weren't going to last. I started panicking. I started insisting about babies and one night I told him I was going to let myself get pregnant regardless of what he said. I said I had it all arranged. I said if he wouldn't take time out of his life for a family then I was going to give up work or go into general practice part time and bring up our children properly.

'For the first time Luke didn't tell me it was too soon or that we'd discuss it again in a few years. He didn't even argue back. He just said he thought it was plain now that we'd be better off apart, wished me a happy life, packed and left. The next week when I was at work he came back and got the rest of his books and clothes. Two days later I got a letter from a lawyer, saying he wanted a divorce. Luke accepted a position in Boston and the next time I saw him was last Monday night at Harry's reception.'

Her hands were shaking too much to pick up her fork to sample any of the second round of dishes that had been delivered, but she thought she managed a fairly creditable smile.

'So that's it, really,' she said jerkily. 'That's the whole, sad, sordid history. But I still haven't told you the most pathetic thing, and that's that every time I see some poor woman at work smile at him invitingly I feel like ripping her head off.

'Don't laugh,' she groaned, when Geoffrey did. 'It's not funny, it's a nightmare.'

'You must still be in love with him.'

Annabel already knew that. She closed her eyes. 'Despite our personal differences, I'll always respect Luke and I have huge admiration for him professionally,' she said quietly. 'That'll never change. He's an incredibly dedicated and inspiring doctor and teacher. And I still remember the good times with him and they were so good it hurts me to think about them. But the bad was pretty bad and he thinks I'm ugly now.'

'He doesn't think you're ugly.'

'Oh, yes, he does.' She blinked her eyes open. 'He told me so tonight.'

'He lied.'

'He never does.'

'Then you misunderstood. You don't exactly make the best of yourself, Annabel, but you're still a gorgeous woman.'

'Thank you for being kind, but I know what he said,' Annabel responded quietly. 'He called me an uptight, screwed-up, frustrated zombie.'

Geoffrey sent her a shocked look and choked on the fried calamari he was eating, but once she'd thumped him on the back and passed him his water and he'd collected himself, she realised he was laughing again.

Annabel studied him. 'I wouldn't be finding it amusing if I were you,' she advised. 'Luke seems to have got the idea in his head that you're the right man to save me from a life of dried up old spinsterhood.'

Geoffrey sobered immediately and Annabel saw a red flush creep up from his neck to his forehead. 'Ah, Annabel. Yes. Actually, I wanted to talk to you about that tonight. I wanted to let you know I wouldn't be pestering you to go out with me any more because I, er, asked Miriam Frost out last weekend.'

'Miriam Frost?' Annabel echoed, astonishment turning her mood from self-pity to shock. She'd been dropping heavy hints about the paediatric charge nurse's interest in Geoffrey for over a year and as far as she'd known he'd never taken any notice. 'And?'

'And we went to a show on Saturday night and had a very pleasant evening,' he said sheepishly. 'Then on Sunday we drove to Kew and walked all around and we're taking a picnic to Hampstead this weekend.'

'I'm very pleased,' she said heartily. 'That's great, Geoffrey. I really like Miriam. She's lovely.'

'You don't mind, then?'

'Of course not. I have a feeling things will work out very well for you.' She did feel a thin, sudden pang of loneliness but that was neither his fault nor his responsibility and she reached out and squeezed his plump arm reassuringly. 'I'm happy about it. She's been keen on you for ages.'

'Can't imagine why,' he mumbled, but she saw his blush deepen and smiled.

'You're a very nice man,' she said firmly. 'A very, very nice man.'

An hour later, hugging her knees to her chest in bed, the calculating part of Annabel's brain, remembering her earlier fears about remaining for ever alone and childless, wondered if she'd made a mistake in never encouraging Geoffrey. Despite her denials to Luke of Geoffrey's seriousness, she sensed she might have been able to interest him if she'd been more receptive.

But inwardly her senses revolted against the thought of marriage ever being an emotional compromise. The truth was that she wanted it all, she acknowledged. For her to marry again she'd need everything she'd had with Luke.

Love, craving, passion, need, all of it. All of it except the pain.

The ringing of the telephone beside her bed brought her out from beneath the covers and she reached for the receiver quickly, expecting it to be one of the nurses on J ward about Daisy. Even when she wasn't on call she regularly left instructions to be called directly about problems with her own patients and such calls came fairly regularly.

Only it wasn't the ward, and the voice that answered her husky acknowledgement and set her pulses thudding had an American accent. 'You're home,' Luke observed unnecessarily. 'How did it go with Clancy? Are you alone?'

'Of course.' Annabel struggled up into a sitting position. 'How's Daisy?'

'Stable.' He sounded amused and Annabel's teeth gritted as it occurred to her that even a marginally recovered Daisy might have done something characteristically outrageous to earn that.

'What's so funny, Luke? Did you have to fight her off?'

'She's only little,' Luke countered easily. 'It wasn't much effort and the fact that she could muster the energy to even try was a good sign. Tell me about your date.'

'What makes you think I went?' she prevaricated, her voice sharpening with irritation with herself for feeling pathetically jealous of her own, critically ill patient and with Luke for calling her and thus offering her the provocation.

'This is the first time you've answered your phone all evening. I've been calling since nine,' he added, making her blink with surprise. 'How was the movie?'

'We didn't get there. Geoffrey found out we were married,' she added quickly, still finding the thought of him checking up on her disconcerting. 'He saw Abdul and Louise Faddoul. He trained with them years ago at Guy's and they asked about you.'

'And?'

'And he was very surprised,' she said shortly. 'Luke, don't go on about Geoffrey any more. He's not interested in me and he's seeing another woman. He only asked me out tonight so he could tell me about it. He sounds very excited about her.'

'Ah, Annie.' He made a soft sound. 'So I was wrong. Do you want me to apologise?'

'Definitely.' She wriggled down in the bed again, pulling a pillow across so she could rest on two, then she folded her free arm under her head and gazed around her room. 'You were horrible to me tonight. You were pushy and rude and horrible and it was all wasted because he doesn't even want me. I was lying here, feeling a bit sorry for myself for a few minutes, but that's just silly. Miriam will be much better for him than I would ever be. And this bedroom isn't so bad, you know. It was unfair of you to call it a horror. I know it's a bit impersonal but I like it. It's very restful.'

'You're already in bed?'

'What do you expect when you ring me at…' she squinted at the clock '…eleven-thirty at night. I was almost asleep.'

He went quiet for a few seconds then said, 'That's early for you.'

'Not these days.' Her fist tightened around the receiver and she lowered her eyes, remembering how it had been once between them. On the nights they'd been at home together when neither of them had been on call they'd rarely made it to sleep until the middle of the night. If all had been well they'd made love, and if they'd been fighting then that had merely added an emotional charge to their passion.

'After seeing Abdul and Louise tonight, on the way home I was thinking about that week we spent in Rhodes,' she revealed huskily, speaking fast to overcome her sudden self-consciousness. They'd bought the seven-day package at the last minute from a travel agent close to the hospital, only to realise in the queue for the airport bus on the final day that Abdul and Louise had been on the same holiday at the same resort and they hadn't even noticed them.

'Do you remember trying to teach me to windsurf that day? I was terrible and you were getting so cross with me but I couldn't stop laughing and my arms were all weak and I kept falling off.'

'That would have been on the one day of the whole week we actually left the hotel room,' he said quietly.

'Really?' Annabel blushed hotly, striving for insouciance, although as soon as he'd reminded her she remembered everything. 'Oh,' she said roughly. 'How silly we were. What a waste that was. I'll have to go back one day and see the island properly.'

'If you feel that strongly there are several places you'll have to go back to,' Luke murmured. 'We didn't see much of Paris.'

Annabel closed her eyes weakly. 'Or Amsterdam,' she whispered. They'd flown to the Dutch capital one weekend when they'd found themselves both unexpectedly off duty together. She'd wanted to see a special exhibition at the Rijksmuseum, but instead, once again, they'd barely ventured out of the hotel room. In those early days, given the hours they'd both been working in London, long stretches of free hours together away from the hospital had been like joyous, incredible treats for them.

'Barcelona,' Luke said softly.

Annabel shivered, remembering the three days over their first Easter when they'd managed to get days off together to go away to Spain. But then, realising abruptly what the memories were doing to her, what she was allowing his voice to do, what he probably knew very well he was doing to her, she rolled over and wordlessly slammed the receiver back onto its rest.

CHAPTER EIGHT

DAISY, still a little puffy and wheezy, greeted Annabel's mock-stern look with a giggle the next morning. 'Oh, no,' she groaned lightly. 'He complained about me.'

'You can't be too sick if you're already making a play for our new professor,' Annabel said coolly, rolling her eyes at Hannah who promptly started to laugh beside her.

'Thought you were still head over heels with your footballer?' Hannah teased.

'I am.' Still giggling, Daisy lifted one frail shoulder. 'He's lovely. He's coming in to see me this morning and he's going to sign autographs for the kids in the children's wards. Dr Stuart, I only tried to kiss him.' The words had made her breathless again, Annabel noted, and she waited quietly while Daisy paused for a moment and collected herself. 'Just a little kiss. To thank him. Only I got…carried away by the drama of the moment. He looked a bit startled, but he didn't mind too much, did he?'

'He'd be used to it,' Hannah said lightly, before Annabel could muster a suitably phrased reply. 'A man like that. He'd have women falling over themselves to get to him. If you want to know the truth, I wouldn't mind kissing him myself.'

Daisy's mouth formed a shocked 'O' and even Mark, their normally sanguine SHO, looked startled. Annabel sent her registrar a brief, annoyed look. 'Do you mind not encouraging her, please?' she said shortly. 'She's incorrigible enough as it is.'

Daisy giggled again and Hannah just laughed. 'With men

114

like that, I wish I were incorrigible,' the younger doctor said lightly. 'Pity I'm just all talk.'

Pity *all* women weren't, Annabel thought coldly.

'How's your heart, Daisy?' After another impatient glance at Hannah, Annabel put on her best consultant expression. 'Did you sleep?'

'I got a bit breathless about five and the registrar came and gave me another shot of diuretic, I think,' Daisy revealed. 'I didn't really sleep. Mr Grant's already been to see me this morning before he had to go to Theatre. He's going to call you later.'

That suggested Luke must have warned the transplant surgeon about Daisy's admission, Annabel registered, nodding as she picked up the charts from the end of the bed. The amount of urine Daisy had passed after the diuretic the evening before and again during the night, as well as the drop in her weight this morning, meant that the medication Luke had prescribed had rid Daisy's body of much of the excess fluid her inefficient heart had allowed to build up.

Annabel examined Daisy thoroughly then made minor adjustments to her drug chart. ECGs, or cardiographs, were done as standard procedure every morning on all her patients at St Peter's, but she asked Mark to organise blood tests and Hannah to ECHO Daisy again in the afternoon. 'You're going to be with us till the end of the week at the very least,' she warned Daisy. 'Your chest X-ray hasn't cleared up as quickly as last time. Have you tried walking yet?'

'It was a bit tough, getting to the bathroom this morning,' Daisy admitted. 'I got almost to the door but then I got a bit weak and breathless and the nurse had to come and help me with a chair.'

'That should improve,' Annabel told her calmly. 'Hopefully, in the meantime, it'll mean the poor nurses won't find you racing a motorbike around the hospital car park.'

'It's a Harley.' Daisy's face brightened and she giggled again. 'John says when I get my new heart he's going to buy me a bike too, then we'll ship them out to Australia and ride around the whole country together.'

'Poor Australia,' Annabel said lightly. 'We should start warning them now.'

Directly after her round she rang Tony Grant, luckily catching him in Theatres between cases. 'Yes, Luke spoke to me last night about her,' he said, after confirming he'd examined Daisy that morning. 'He was also concerned about her but you know her best, Annabel. What do you think?'

'I'd say she has weeks rather than months,' Annabel admitted quietly. 'Her personality's so sparkly it's easy to be deceived, but physically she's deteriorated alarmingly over the past month. We'll get her out of hospital this time but this might be one of the last times we do. Her blood gases last night were the worst they've ever been and they're not all that much better this morning. She's going to need oxygen at home this time.'

'There's not much happening at my end at present,' the surgeon said heavily. 'Hopefully I'll be in touch soon.'

Hopefully. When their conversation finished Annabel put down the telephone slowly and buried her face in her hands.

'Trouble at mill?' Geoffrey's cheery voice interrupted her reverie and she lifted her head and grimaced at him.

'We had to readmit Daisy Miller last night,' she explained. 'She's not doing particularly well and Tony doesn't sound overly optimistic about the chances of us getting her a heart any time soon.'

'How's she holding up?'

'Bright as a button as usual,' Annabel admitted. 'She

can't even walk to the door of her room this morning but she's talking about heading off on a Harley Davidson around Australia with her new boyfriend.'

Geoffrey laughed. 'Sounds like Daisy,' he agreed. 'I'll keep my fingers crossed for her. Coming to St Joseph's?'

Annabel checked her watch quickly and nodded, pushing her chair back from the desk to go with him. He suddenly let out a soft whistle and she looked up at him in surprise, then promptly blushed when she realised his eyes had dropped.

'Geoffrey!' she chided, wrapping her doctor's coat around her to conceal her knees. 'They're just legs. Don't stare.'

'It's the first time I've ever seen them,' he protested, his eyes dancing. 'I was beginning to think you didn't have any.'

'It's just an old outfit I found in my wardrobe,' she murmured self-consciously. 'It's years since I've worn it. Since it's supposed to be warm today I thought it'd be nice to try something cooler.'

By her old standards the yellow outfit, with matching slim-fitting sleeveless tunic and skirt, had been conservative—she had vague memories of originally buying the outfit because she'd fallen in love with the colour rather than the style—and the skirt, at barely an inch above her knees, was hardly short.

But, given she rarely wore anything above her lower calves these days, she had been feeling a little bit uncomfortable. She'd been worried the colour clashed with her hair or that she might look like mutton dressed up as lamb, but Geoffrey's apparent approval lifted her confidence fractionally.

'You suit a bit of colour,' he told her appraisingly, his

eyes twinkling as he opened the stairwell door for her. 'You
look lovely.'

'Thank you.' She wasn't sure she believed him but even
the small boost to her ego of him noticing helped. Feeling
herself still blushing, Annabel rushed ahead of him. Now
she thought about it, she rarely wore a lot of colour these
days, she realised. Beige and creams, of course, and black,
and she had one navy suit. She'd given away a lot of things
around the time of her divorce to charity shops but there
were still a few old favourites lurking about the house.

Tonight, if she wasn't busy on call, she vowed, she'd go
through the attic and the spare room's wardrobe and draw-
ers properly and see what else she'd saved from years ago.
Perhaps she'd been rather silly, changing her appearance
so drastically after Luke. She couldn't properly remember
now why it had seemed so important at the time that she
dress more sedately. Perhaps there were more clothes she
could make use of now. And the same hairstyle could be
boring after so many years. Perhaps she should let it grow
a little again.

It was only the end of April, but in line with the weather
forecaster's predictions on the radio that morning summer
seemed to have arrived early. In her ten-minute lunch-break
between her teaching session and the start of her clinic she
met Harry outside in the hospital grounds for a chat over
a sandwich in the sun.

Although in semi-retirement since Luke's arrival, Harry
still planned to attend meetings and his Wednesday clinic
every week. 'Luke seems to have taken over rather
smoothly,' he mused, his complacent air suggesting he was
happy to take full credit for the success of his replacement.
'The new budget was approved last weekend. He just faced
up to the trust, refused to compromise and pushed until they
gave in. I believe he's going to be very, very good for St

Peter's. I only hope we can keep him here long term. What's your impression, Annabel?'

She sent him a wan look. 'I miss you.'

'Oh, you'll forget me soon enough. New broom and all that. It was time someone shook things up around here.' But Harry looked pleased.

If it was shaking Harry wanted then he couldn't have chosen a better man than Luke for the job, Annabel thought quietly, but she confined her response to a mute shrug.

What she couldn't put off, though, once her afternoon clinic was over, was trying to speak to Luke herself. As usual on a Wednesday, the session had gone on far longer than it should have and she was late getting away so she was expecting to have to get Luke's telephone number at his hotel from Switchboard. But one of the nurses in Outpatients mentioned she'd seen him walking through the area shortly before the end of Annabel's clinic so Annabel made her reluctant way up to Harry's old office in case she could catch him.

The door was closed and she knocked on it automatically, but his command to come in startled her a little because she hadn't really expected him to be there. She opened the door hesitantly, then stilled as she saw that the high leather back of his chair was swivelled away from her. He was talking on the telephone. He swung around in his chair, saw her, frowned in a distracted sort of way then motioned for her come in and wait, before swinging back towards the window again.

'Yes,' he said quietly, to whoever he was talking to. 'Fine.'

Flushing at the disturbing memory of their own telephone conversation the night before, Annabel ignored the signal he'd sent her directing her to the chair in front of his desk, and instead took a couple of shaky steps over to

Harry's old bookshelves. She cast a quick eye over the stacks of titles, surprised to find that Luke had yet to make any changes to the collection of outdated journals and old textbooks Harry had found so hard to throw away.

Whomever he was talking to clearly had a lot to say, she noted. The conversation was definitely one-sided, with Luke's occasional contributions confined to the odd murmur or monosyllabic response, but then he said quietly, 'Next Saturday, then. Good. I'll organise it. I'll let you know the details and I'll collect you at Heathrow.' Annabel heard a very feminine expression of gratitude from the other end.

Annabel stared fixedly at Harry's shelves while the conversation ended—efficiently, thank God, with fondness but without any of the extended farewells and kisses and prolonged declarations of love she'd been steeling herself for—and when she heard the sound of Luke replacing the telephone she turned around slowly and met his quiet look head on, her expression rigid.

'Girlfriend, was it?' she asked in a brittle voice. 'I must say I was surprised when Harry first mentioned you were coming to London alone. Decided to wait until you were settled, before following you, did she? Is she staying permanently or is this just a quick visit first to see how she likes the place?'

'I was talking to my mother,' Luke said neutrally. 'It's twenty years next week since my father died and she's coming to spend some time at his grave. You look good.'

Annabel, abruptly self-conscious, folded her arms across her chest and lowered her head. 'It's old.' She dismissed his comment raggedly, refusing to admit that his criticism the night before might have had anything to do with her change of style. 'I'm sorry,' she muttered. 'I'm sorry about your father. How is Rosemary these days?'

'Sentimental.'

'It's a good time of year for her to visit. I mean, not because of your father but because of the weather. It's not too cold at least now—'

'Is there a point,' Luke interrupted before she could finish, 'to this visit, Annabel? Or has our relationship advanced to the stage of enjoying social calls now?'

Annabel dropped her eyes. 'I wanted to ask your help with Daisy,' she told him after a few seconds. 'I'm worried by how fast she's deteriorating and I'd appreciate the chance to talk through her case in detail with you. I'd like you to review my management. I want to make sure I'm not missing something. I want to be certain there isn't something else I could be doing for her.'

'I'll need to see X-rays and ECHOs, as well as admission and outpatient notes from the time of her diagnosis.'

She nodded. 'Of course.' There was no other way he could do a thorough review. 'Her notes are about three feet thick but I've got them all, and any films not on the ward are in my office. She was referred directly to my predecessor here when she was fifteen.'

'Bring everything up, then.'

'You mean now?' It was late and the sort of review she was suggesting could take hours. She'd expected him to appoint a time in the next day or two.

'Why not? Paperwork can wait.' His white coat and suit jacket were slung over the other chair in the room, and now he unbuttoned the cuffs of his shirt with the air of a man settling down to business. 'You're not off home yet, are you? Aren't you on call tonight?'

'You're not,' she reminded him, swallowing heavily as his movements revealed a strong and familiar hair-roughened forearm. 'Luke, Daisy's not going to change overnight. I'm just grateful you're willing to do this. We

can leave it till tomorrow. You must be tired after last night.
I'm sure you're anxious to get home.'

'To a hotel room television and mini-bar?' he asked ironically. 'Relax, Annabel. I think I can pass on them for a
couple more hours.'

Annabel stared at him. It hadn't occurred to her until
then that he might be lonely. Not Luke. Never Luke. 'But
you know loads of people in London,' she exclaimed. 'You
must have dozens of friends wanting to catch up with you.
Why on earth are you still staying in a hotel if you don't
want to?'

'Convenience.' He finished rolling his second sleeve, and
against the white of his shirt his arms looked tanned and
healthy. She seemed to be having trouble dragging her eyes
away from them. 'I'm putting in long hours at present,' he
continued. 'At the hotel I'm only five minutes away from
here. Once I'm settled I'll start looking for something permanent.'

'Look, if it's that horrible there—' She broke off, nib-
bling at her lower lip, sure she was going to be letting
herself in for more heartache than she could live with but
still not quite able to stop herself. 'Luke, you could stay at
the house until Rosemary arrives.'

She'd met Luke's glamorous mother when she'd flown
over from America for their wedding and she'd liked her
at the time, although—considering the divorce—she would
be too nervous about meeting Luke's mother again to have
her stay at the house.

'It's almost as convenient and it's not as if there isn't
room. I'm on call all weekend and I was planning to spend
most of my time in here, doing paperwork. Also, if I'm not
needed here on Saturday night I've got a fund-raising dinner to attend. You'd have the place to yourself. I know it's
not luxurious and I know you don't exactly approve of the

decor, but at least you know it and it's not as impersonal as a hotel.'

To her relief, Luke, rather than mocking her offer, merely looked puzzled. 'Are you feeling sorry for me?'

'Perhaps a little.' When he smiled she found herself imitating the movement. 'Believe me, that's a very strange feeling,' she admitted faintly. 'One I'm not at all used to. But I'm serious, Luke.'

Morally, as opposed to legally, she still felt as if part of the house belonged to him. He'd paid for it. The terms of their settlement had been embarrassingly generously weighted in her favour, and the money her solicitor had agreed she had to pay him had seemed trivial once she'd realised, a few years later, the true worth of the house. She spread her hands. 'I've made the offer. It's up to you whether you accept it.'

Luke leaned back in his chair and studied her steadily. 'You're a peculiar little creature at times, Annie.'

'I thought you thought I was peculiar all the time,' she murmured. She felt breathless suddenly. It seemed wise to retreat to the door. 'I'll just run down and fetch Daisy's notes. It shouldn't take me long.'

But there were enough notes and X-rays to mean she needed two trips so, leaving Luke to study some of Daisy's very earliest films, she went back for the second lot, including the notes on the ward. She'd already checked with Daisy to ensure she had no objections to her discussing her case with Luke, and while she was on J she called in on her patient to see how she was.

'Much, much better,' Daisy assured her heartily, although Annabel could see from the end of the bed that, despite the oxygen she was still receiving via two little prongs beneath her nose, there'd been little improvement in either her colour or her chart.

'Mr Grant came to see me after lunch,' Daisy went on, referring to her transplant surgeon. She struggled up a little higher in her bed and giggled. 'If you ask me, Dr Stuart, he wasn't that interested in me. He sort of prodded me about a bit and looked at my X-ray, but what he really wanted to do was talk to John. He brought a football in for him to sign for his son.'

'Whom he no doubt forgot to mention is not even seven weeks old yet,' Annabel revealed with a smile. 'I think we both know who Tony wanted the autograph for.'

'That's what I thought, too.' Daisy rolled her eyes. 'Honestly. Men! They're so pathetic sometimes, aren't they?' Her voice was still wheezy and she still had to keep stopping every few words to catch her breath, but Annabel thought there'd been a little improvement in that since the morning. 'I may be only twenty but, I tell you, I can see right through them. Professor Geddes is different, though. Do you think he'll come back and see me when he's looked at all my stuff?'

'Now, Daisy,' Annabel warned, but the younger woman merely giggled at her again.

'I won't jump all over him,' she teased, her eyes dancing. 'Or at least not until I've got enough energy to put up a better fight if he tries to get away again. And he is a little old for me—you're right about that. But he's still delicious to look at and I liked him and I hope I haven't frightened him off for all time.'

'Frightening Luke would take more than a poppet like you,' Annabel assured her dryly. To frighten Luke away Daisy would have to have turned into a harridan like she herself was, and Annabel couldn't see that happening in a hurry. 'I suspect he will come and see you again but perhaps not till tomorrow.'

'Actually, Dr Stuart, I was just thinking that *you* and

Professor Geddes look good together,' Daisy said innocently. 'Do you like him?'

'He's an excellent physician,' Annabel said neutrally. 'Deep breaths, Daisy.' She drew her stethoscope out. 'Another breath in.' She examined Daisy's heart and chest briefly and elected to continue her current treatment, including the dopamine infusion into the venflon Luke had inserted the night before. 'Hannah and I are on call tonight. If you're feeling worse or there's anything you need just ask one of the nurses to bleep us.'

By the time she got back up to Harry's old office, Luke had Daisy's earliest X-rays up on the screen on the far wall and several sets of notes spread open on the desk in front of him. 'I can't find her initial heart biopsy results,' he said when Annabel put down the load she was carrying on one of the chairs. He searched though a couple of pages, sounding preoccupied.

'I see there's a note here on a verbal report on one in your handwriting so that must have been when you were a registrar, but I can't find the official histology. Did you rely on just one biopsy or did you repeat it?'

'We did another two years ago, the first time she went into failure,' Annabel told him, looking through the notes she'd just retrieved to try and find it. 'Just in case we'd missed something with the first one. Here's this one.'

She passed across the blue report for him to read then took over the notes he'd been searching through to see if she could find the original biopsy result. 'Neither showed any inflammation or viral particles,' she murmured. 'Here it is.' Having found what he'd been looking for, she slid that across the desk, too. 'They're pretty similar.'

'And her first presenting symptoms were fatigue on exercise at school?'

'She stopped being able to play hockey,' Annabel confirmed. 'Until she was about fifteen she was brilliant at sport. She represented her school and district at sprinting for several years and she was captain of the school's first hockey team. Until she had to give up all sport, the school had been confident she had the talent to go even as far as national-level hockey. She found herself losing stamina and growing gradually weaker. She had to withdraw from games and her aunt took her to her GP who noticed her heart was large. He did a few preliminary investigations, including an ECG, which was abnormal, then sent her immediately to us.'

'*Aunt?*' Luke questioned.

'Daisy's parents died before she was five,' Annabel explained. 'We don't know for sure,' she added, in response to his sharply enquiring look, 'but we don't think so. Her father was killed in some sort of chemical explosion at work and her mother died six months later aged twenty-nine.

'Daisy says it was accidental but Caroline—that's Daisy's aunt and her mother's sister—has hinted there was an overdose involved. There's no known history of cardiac disease with either of them. Daisy was an only child. There's no other family on her father's side and I've screened her aunt and her four children and their children and found nothing.'

'I see things were fairly stable with Daisy for the first two and a half years.'

'She was able to finish college,' Annabel confirmed. 'She's always been bright so even when she needed time in hospital she didn't seem to have any trouble catching up. She went into heart failure for the first time soon after her eighteenth birthday, and that's when we referred her for transplant. We realised then that her disease was going to be rapidly progressive. She's been waiting two years now.

As you saw on Tuesday, we've lost the luxury of being able to wait much longer.'

'Who did this one?' Luke drew out Daisy's initial ECHO pictures. 'You?'

Annabel shook her head and checked the initials along the bottom of the scan. 'My predecessor,' she explained. She moved quickly out of the way as Luke swung out of his chair and came round to put up another X-ray. 'That scan was done before I came here as a registrar.'

Working together, they moved methodically though Daisy's history and serial tests from the time of that first scan to her latest presentation, taking the information from the notes where it was available with Luke questioning Annabel when he needed to.

At the end of that, after almost an hour and a half of thorough, detailed examination, looking at every small piece of information, every chart, X-ray, ECG and ECHO result, he took Daisy's ECG from that day, studied it, then sat back in his chair and regarded Annabel steadily.

Annabel tensed. 'I've missed something,' she said huskily, trying to read his expression. 'Haven't I?'

Instead of answering that, he merely said quietly, 'What made you choose cardiology in the end, Annie? When we were married you used to talk as if you were determined to go either into your father's general practice or give up medicine altogether.'

She blinked a little. 'Temporarily,' she agreed. 'But that was because I wanted to have children. Since I was thinking about giving up work for a few years I decided that finding a job afterwards would be easier with some training in general practice behind me, rather than just hospital medicine.

'But I was always more interested in hearts. I found your enthusiasm for the field and your teaching incredibly inspiring. Obviously, when the time came for me to make real decisions about my career I was single again and I didn't have to think about the best way to raise a family. I could do what I wanted and I did.'

'Have you given any thought to completing a doctorate?'

'A PhD?' She blinked at him. 'Oh, Luke,' she exclaimed mildly. 'Of course not. I'm quite content where I am, thank you very much. I don't harbour any secret ambition to conquer the scientific world. I'm not like you. I don't want great trails of letters after my name and I'm very happy being a little cog around this place.'

'But no regrets about your choice of career?'

'None.' Although if their lives had worked out the way she'd once hoped she'd have been very happy combining general practice and a family. 'Why?' She sat back in her chair and folded her arms nervously. 'Should I have regrets?'

'Not according to this.' He moved his hand to indicate the now disordered stacks of notes. 'Your management of Daisy has been nothing short of world class. You haven't missed anything, Annie. On the contrary, you've been extraordinarily diligent and thorough. I might have done one or two things differently.

'At Brigham I'd have been more interventionist at the time of first diagnosis,' he said, referring, she knew, to the hospital he'd worked at in Boston, 'because, for better or worse, that's the way we operated there. I'd certainly have wanted to include her in some of the trials we were running. Some of my drug choices might have been subtly different, but they're the only differences. In the long term I doubt they'd have changed anything. There's no magic bullet here.

'In my opinion, a transplant's been Daisy's only realistic chance for survival for three years now. How long she lives without one is out of our hands.'

Annabel sighed tiredly. She rested right back in her chair, her hands on each arm, and closed her eyes. 'That's what I thought,' she admitted sorrowfully. 'I don't know what to do. I'm relieved you don't think I've missed anything in the past but I still feel inadequate. We should be able to help, Luke.' She opened her eyes and looked directly at him, her frustration unconcealed. 'It's paralysing to realise there's nothing else we can do.'

'How much does she understand?'

'Daisy doesn't miss a thing, but her particular brand of cheery optimism is a precious trait, I think. I tend to let her guide our discussions and she only occasionally asks directly how much time I think she has. But she is aware that things are bad now. We talked seriously a couple of admissions ago when she was worried, and she knows her heart's deteriorated since then. She wrote her will two years ago and Caroline mentioned a few weeks ago that she'd told her she'd updated it.'

She looked down at her hands. 'Heavy stuff for a twenty-year-old,' she said sadly. 'When I was her age I was still a child.'

'I doubt it.' Luke sounded amused. 'I remember you being not so much older and you were light years away from childhood then.'

Annabel looked up swiftly. 'Did I embarrass you then, Luke?'

He tilted his head. 'What are you talking about?'

'Did I embarrass you with the way I used to chase you around the hospital?' she said roughly. 'I've often wondered what your colleagues must have thought about you being pursued so ardently all that year by a little medical student. In those early days all I knew was how desperately I wanted you to notice me. I was too naïve to understand about subtlety and playing it cool. Did your friends find me funny? Did they tease you? I expect they were incredulous when you married me. Did you all secretly laugh about me?'

'Of course not.'

Annabel didn't believe him. 'It's really not necessary to protect me.' Fixing a brittle smile on her face, she retrieved her white coat from where she'd discarded it earlier across a spare chair. She stacked Daisy's files into order and collected as many of the current ones as she could in one armful. 'If you ever agree to acknowledge the truth about our relationship, trust me, I'll cope.'

He frowned at her. 'What are you talking about?'

'It doesn't matter.' She met his narrowed regard with deliberate neutrality. 'I must go. Hannah will be expecting to see me on the ward. Thank you…' she waved at the remaining notes on his desk '…for your help with Daisy. I'll fetch the rest from your secretary tomorrow.'

She pulled the office door shut behind her as she left, but he reached it just after her and called her name before she was even ten yards along the corridor. 'You're wrong about my friends laughing at you,' he said grimly. 'You were a very sexy girl, Annabel. Any one of them would have crawled over broken glass if he'd thought it'd mean getting you into bed.'

'What a pity you were never so eager,' she said wanly. She turned away. 'Goodnight, Luke.'

CHAPTER NINE

LUKE came to the house the next night. Annabel opened the door without surprise. The shape of him had been obvious through the glass and she'd been half expecting him anyway. 'Have you decided to come and stay?' she asked, looking behind him towards the street. 'Did you bring a suitcase?'

'I left messages with your secretary for you to call me this afternoon.' Ignoring her questions, he walked past her inside, his size immediately making the hallway feel small. 'What happened?'

'Do, please, come in,' she said ironically, sending his broad back a flat look. 'I was held up because my clinic ran over time and I couldn't imagine you needing to talk to me being about anything that couldn't wait until tomorrow.' She followed him into her sitting room. 'I was planning to call you in the morning after my round. I can offer you tea, coffee or juice, but I'm afraid the only alcohol I have is a bottle of chocolate liqueur which one of my patients gave me for Christmas.'

'I'm not thirsty.' He cast a rapid, disparaging look around the room and she saw his eyes focus on the shelf above the gas fire as he registered the absence of the photograph he'd studied on his last visit. 'Contaminated, was it, Annie? Straight into the bin the minute I left?'

'If you're referring to my graduation-day photograph, I posted it to my father,' she said huskily. She hadn't quite been able to bring herself to destroy it. 'He seems to enjoy surrounding himself with memorabilia.'

'A characteristic you clearly don't share,' Luke observed coolly.

'Perhaps my past isn't as pleasant to remember as his is.' She kept her head up and her eyes steadily meeting his. 'Is there a point to this, Luke, or are we having social calls now?'

Her pointed parroting of his comment the evening before seemed to amuse him. 'Quit stressing out,' he commanded softly. 'Perhaps I've come to inspect the accommodation.'

'I'll show you the room.' Now she'd had time for second thoughts, she regretted having made the offer to Luke, but after his help with Daisy she would have felt mean-spirited and churlish withdrawing it. Still, she was keeping her fingers crossed that he'd decide he preferred the comforts of his hotel after all.

Without waiting to see if he followed her, she returned to the door and walked up the stairs. 'I've kept my study and turned your old one into a spare bedroom. I think if you decide to stay you'll find it comfortable. Of course, there's only one bathroom but, as I mentioned, I'm expecting to be at St Peter's most of the weekend.'

He did follow her, and when she opened the bedroom door and stepped back he walked past her and inside. He looked around at the unremarkable decor and bedroom furnishings with a neutral expression. 'What happened to the desk?'

'Sold to a junk shop.' The antique bureau had been in superb condition and she knew he'd loved it, but at the time she'd wanted to get rid of it. There'd been no room in her life for sentimentality.

'Such an unemotional little creature you've turned yourself into,' he accused softly. 'What did you mean with that crack last night?'

'I was curious,' answered Annabel sharply. 'Oh, I'm sure

your friends were suitably circumspect once you actually married me, but I've often imagined the way you all must have laughed about me being so mad for you in the beginning.'

'I told you last night, no one laughed.' He put his hands behind him and braced them on the doorhandle, the movement disturbingly highlighting the strong outline of his thighs beneath the trousers of his immaculate dark suit. 'I told you what they thought of you.'

'Broken glass,' she remembered. 'Yes.' But she didn't believe him.

'You think it was easy for me, keeping my hands off you back then?'

'You didn't seem to find it particularly difficult.'

'It was hell.'

'Liar.' She met his flat green gaze without flinching. 'I threw myself at you for almost a year before you deigned to even notice.'

'The way you used that soft little voice on me used to put my temperature up five degrees,' he said roughly. 'The way you used to corner me and press yourself against me, trying to kiss me, begging me to touch you, drove me practically out of my mind that year. I wanted you but I held off, Annie.' His eyes bored into hers. 'I kept you at a distance for *your* sake, not mine. I didn't want you distracted. I wanted to see you through your exams and qualified. If you think any of that was easy for me, you're nuts.'

'Your memories are distorted,' she countered swiftly. 'Do you think I'm still so fragile I can't face the truth?'

'What truth?' He moved abruptly, sending her recoiling in fright, but he merely registered her movement with grim amusement then strode away from her towards the window on the opposite side of the room. He braced his arms against the sill and half sat against it, his expression brood-

ing. 'The truth according to your warped memory of it—
or reality?'

'You never wanted me,' Annabel said crisply. She came
a few feet into the room, leaned one hip against the wall,
crossed her ankles and folded her arms defiantly. 'You gave
in because you were so sick of me chasing you, and you
offered to marry me because you felt guilty you'd taken
my virginity. I didn't expect it, you know. I mean, I longed
for that, but to me then that was like longing for the moon.
I never expected it to happen. I realise you probably felt
as if it was the right thing to do but you shouldn't have felt
obliged. Were you shocked when I said yes?'

'No. And your virginity wasn't a surprise to me.' His
eyes narrowed. 'Why else did you think I waited so long
to take it away from you?'

'As I said, you never wanted me. Or at least never in the
way I wanted you.' Her mouth tightened. 'You gave in
because I'd been pestering you for so long that you were
sick of me and it was my graduation and you knew how
much I craved you so out of some misguided spirit of al-
truistic kindness you decided to give me a present.'

'For heaven's sake, Annie.' He swung abruptly upright
again and she tensed, forcing herself to hold her ground
this time lest she amuse him again, but he merely turned
away from her to stare out the window.

'Even from you, I've never heard anything so insane. I
have never wanted any woman the way I wanted you. I
only had to think of you to—' He broke off abruptly. 'Remember how it was when we were eventually together,' he
ordered. 'I couldn't keep my hands off you. I couldn't come
near you without touching you. Remember that and tell me
again that all that time you think I was forcing myself.'

'We were married,' she said roughly. 'You knew how

much I loved you and you decided to make the best of it. You felt obliged to keep me happy—'

'*Obliged?* You're mad.' He turned around again and glared at her. 'What was last week about, then?' he demanded savagely. 'You think I felt obliged again when I tore off your clothes and went for your breasts, Annie? Hmm? Do you think I did that because I felt obliged?'

'Why did you do that?' she demanded hoarsely. 'You make sense of it, then. Why did you do that?'

'Work it out for yourself.'

The hurtful thing was that she could. She could work it out. 'You felt sorry for me because I'm so ugly now,' she cried.

'*Ugly?*' Luke scowled. 'Where the hell did that come from?'

'You said—'

'I said you were repressed and frustrated, and you are. Physically, you're an attractive woman, Annabel. Once you enjoyed that but now you cover yourself up so no man can see you properly and you live the life of a celibate. I was trying to wake you up to yourself. I hate seeing you like this.'

'What, happy?' she countered swiftly.

'Bitter.' The gaze that raked her was hard and green and utterly without compromise. 'Emotionally neutered and frightened and embittered. What happened to you, Annabel? What happened to change you so much? Were you...? Did someone do something bad to you?'

She stared up at him. 'What?'

'Did someone *attack* you?'

'*What?*'

He frowned. 'I wondered—'

'Don't,' she said faintly. 'Don't wonder. No one attacked me. But someone *hurt* me, Luke.' There was concern but no knowledge in his face, and she knew he was still light years away from understanding. 'You've got no idea, have you?' She couldn't believe it. She couldn't believe he didn't understand.

'Luke, *you* hurt me. Don't you understand yet? I didn't marry you because you were good in bed. I married you because I *loved* you. You were my world, but to you I was simply an inconvenience, standing in the way of your ambitions and your career, and one night you packed and left me and I never saw you again.'

'*I* did this?' He lifted one hand towards her, his face utterly drained of colour now, but when she turned her face away from him she saw the movement of his arm dropping. '*Me?*'

'The other day, when I told you I picked myself up quickly and went back to work?' she reminded him huskily. 'I lied. Losing you just about killed me. I did go back to work that Monday but only because I had to and because work was the only way I could keep functioning. I'm sorry I've offended you, by not bouncing back from that with some great long triumphant procession of lovers and babies, but my feelings for you were never quite as insubstantial as yours for me. I went off sex the same night you went off me.'

'What are you talking about?' he demanded rawly. 'You might have shed a nostalgic tear or two but—'

'It doesn't matter.' She shook her head, then looked back at him, pleased by the stark pallor of his skin because that told her she'd shocked him and he deserved to be shocked. But, still, it wasn't in her nature to deliberately inflict pain. 'You needn't worry too much,' she said eventually. 'You didn't drive me round the twist or anything. I didn't try to slit my wrists or jump off any bridges. And I got over it.'

'Your father said you barely blinked—'

He broke off, but Annabel had heard him. 'You spoke to Daddy about me?' she asked hoarsely.

'Frequently, in the months after I left. He said you were fine.' He looked sick. 'He was unhappy about the divorce plans but he didn't think there was a problem on your side. He said you'd told him it was a relief to be free to live your own life again.'

'I said that so he wouldn't worry. He was upset enough already, you see, and I didn't want to add to that. I pretended I didn't really mind too much.'

'But you knew it was over, Annabel. You told me over and over that if Boston was that important to me I could just go alone. You didn't seem to care. The night I left you told me if I refused you a child there would be no reason to stay together. I thought that meant you were admitting we had nothing left, that you weren't in love with me any more. And you were talking about leaving medicine and that would have been disastrous for you. I have never doubted that separating then was the right thing for both of us.'

'Now you're the one putting words into my mouth,' she whispered. 'I was angry because I knew you still resented me for saying no to America. And I wanted a child because I desperately wanted your baby, as well as because I thought that would keep you with me. I could tell you were restless and it seemed as if there were so many women ready to step in and...I felt insecure.'

'Everything I said, you fought against me,' he said hoarsely. 'Annie, it wasn't just the fundamental things like where we should live or whether it was the right time for a baby—it was everything in our lives. You'd disagree over even the simple things, like whose turn it was to do chores or what night we should visit your father. You argued with me on principle. I could see no other reason but that you regretted marrying so soon and you wanted your freedom.'

'I wanted you to see me as an equal,' she argued. 'If I didn't fight I thought you'd lose respect and walk all over me. I wanted you to recognise me as an individual, as your partner, and not just a silly child who'd manipulated you into a marriage you never wanted.'

'But I already saw you as an equal. You were my wife. Why didn't you tell me how you felt at the time?'

'I tried to,' she protested. 'Or at least I used to try to, but you'd get so frustrated that I was disagreeing with you that you'd stop listening and drag me to bed instead, and for a little while everything would seem all right—only later it would all start over again.'

'I'm sorry.' She'd walked slowly towards him and now he turned to her and took her face between her hands and kissed her gently. 'I'm sorry, Annie. If I'd known...' He didn't finish that. 'I didn't mean to hurt you. I didn't realise I had.'

Annabel stared up at him, her face hot beneath his hands. 'I decided eventually that you did the right thing,' she whispered. 'If you hadn't left I would just have gone on resenting you for not loving me as much as I loved you, and that would have just kept on getting worse.'

He kissed her nose softly. 'But I did love you.'

'In an indulgent, amused-adult sort of way,' she conceded gravely. 'Not the way you're supposed to love the woman you marry. It didn't take me long to realise that, you see, and it hurt. You should never have asked me to marry you, Luke.'

'I didn't want anyone else to have you,' he said huskily.

She froze as finally, finally, she began to understand what might have motivated him. 'You certainly got your way on that,' she said distantly.

'Ah, Annie.' He made a sound, half impatience, half sigh. 'You're wrong to think I wasn't in love with you.' He slid his hands down from her cheeks to her neck and then her shoulders, sparking waves of heat and sending them spreading across her skin. 'I was. You were passionate and loving and generous and responsive. I couldn't look at you and not want you.'

'That's not love, Luke.' She lifted her own hands and put them over his, wanting to hate him for what he'd done but instead finding herself loving the heated scent arising from the column of his throat and the rough texture of his hands against her palms and fingers. 'That's something much more common and far less noble. You wanted me as a possession, like a toy. Then, when you discovered I wasn't an obedient doll who'd always act the way you wanted me to act, you stopped wanting me.'

'Stopped wanting you?' he said, his soft, rasping words stirring her senses as much as his hands were, moving restlessly beneath hers against her shoulders. 'Do you believe that?'

'Isn't it the truth?' she whispered.

'You haunted me for years.' His expression preoccupied now, he ran his hands slowly down the sides of her breasts to her waist then over the soft swell of her hips to her thighs. 'It was years before I could look at another woman and not see you in her place.'

Her chest tightened at the thought of him with anyone at all, but he bent his head and touched his mouth to hers, softly, gently and so benignly that her tension eased and she felt no alarm. She kissed him back, slowly, and just as quietly, offering no resistance as he gently eased her mouth open and kissed him properly.

Annabel dropped her hands and stood there, submissive and trance-like, not objecting as his hands slowly ran over her outline again. When he drew her forward against him, his mouth leaving hers to track across her cheeks to her forehead and to her hair, she laid her face against his throat, breathing in the male-scented warmth of him, taking what comfort she could from their embrace and letting him do what he wanted.

His hands slid restlessly up from the backs of her thighs to cup her bottom, and she lifted herself against him and murmured incoherent words, her body starting to tremble.

'I used to dream about holding you like this.' Luke's fingers stroked the skin between her thighs and the rise of her buttocks repeatedly, probing her flesh through her skirt. His hands spread, cupping and caressing her. 'I used to dream about the way your body curves here.' His hands ran over the shape of her buttocks and dipped to her thighs again. 'Remembering how silky your skin was used to drive me insane.'

Until that moment his touch had been seductively languorous and comforting, a form of quiet physical apology and reconciliation, but then he shifted his body against her, parted her knees and slid one hard thigh between her hers.

The overt, unmistakable sexuality of the movement sent alarm bells clanging in Annabel's head. She recoiled. 'Feeling generous, Luke?' she demanded, remembering how cruelly he'd criticised her the night before. 'Trying to shake me up? Trying to wake me up to myself again?'

She drew back from him strongly. Luke dropped his arms and made no attempt to prevent her but merely watched her, his eyes narrowed, his face unexpectedly flushed and heated, as she backed quickly away from him on trembling legs.

She looked down at her shaking hands disparagingly. 'And there I was, resigned to you being determined not to take on that particular task,' she said jerkily. 'Well, don't

fret on my account. Geoffrey might be out of contention
but I expect if I get desperate enough I'll find some man
eventually. I'd like you to leave now, please,' she added,
when Luke still said nothing, merely stood there, watching
her, with a dangerous glitter in his eyes. 'Naturally you can
consider my invitation to you to stay rescinded.'

'Because we just kissed?' He tilted his head slightly, his
gaze unwavering. 'You're overreacting, aren't you, Annie?
All you had to say was stop.'

'I'm sure your hotel's not as bad as you made it sound,'
she told him feverishly. 'At least not bad enough to warrant
you taking on the harrowing chore of having to make love
to me. Goodnight, Luke.'

'All right, Annabel, have it your way.' When he strode
towards her she pressed herself back against the wall but
he just regarded her impatiently, before walking past her
and down the stairs. 'I'll go.'

However, at the bottom he paused and looked up at her
again. 'I was trying to contact you today because I've been
going over the budgets from this year. Your Wednesday
and Thursday clinics have been running too long every
week. Yesterday was a disgrace. You're costing the hospital money it can't afford in nursing overtime. You've got
two weeks to cut back your numbers or I'll start doing it
for you.'

Then, while she stared at him in mute shock, Luke
merely smiled coldly, opened her front door and walked
out.

'He's threatened to cut my Wednesday clinic,' Annabel told
Geoffrey the next morning, too distraught still from Luke's
autocratic command to handle the issue as discreetly as she
knew she should have. 'Who does he think he is?'

'Your boss?' Geoffrey ventured gingerly.

Annabel blinked. 'Technically, yes,' she conceded finally, 'but we're still supposed to function as independent
consultants. And Harry would never have dreamed of pulling a stunt like this.'

'Which might be why he was forced into retirement.'

'*Forced?*'

'So I heard.'

'But he's been talking about retirement for years.'

'He wanted to stay on as director part time,' Geoffrey
told her. 'But the department's overspent badly the past five
years. Harry didn't have the wherewithal to make cuts
where they were needed and so...' he drew one finger
across his throat evocatively '...he was out.'

'And they shelled out countless hundreds of thousands
of pounds and brought in a hatchet man,' Annabel said
bitterly.

'Hardly.' Geoffrey grinned at her. 'Well, you might be
right about what they had to pay Luke to get him, but if
they'd wanted a hatchet man they'd have appointed an ad-
ministrator, not one of the best physicians in the field.
You're just irritated because you see it as your ex-husband
telling you what to do rather than your boss,' he told her
sagely.

'St Peter's couldn't have got a better successor for Harry.
We should be grateful Luke's ambitious enough to agree
to take on the extra workload of the administrative work at
all—most clinicians of his calibre wouldn't dream of it.
And however much we might disapprove of the politics
behind the rationing of funds, Annabel, we either run to
budget or it's merger at best and closure at worst. You're
the only doctor on staff who isn't full of praise for the job
Luke's doing.'

'I'm not saying he's not good at his job,' Annabel said
tersely. Ambition was something Luke, certainly, had never

been short of. 'Simply that I object to his autocratic way
of doing it. And I don't see why you're in such a bouncy
mood about him. I thought you'd be sympathetic, Geoffrey.
I thought you'd been warned about some of your clinics as
well.'

'We have been through a couple of my lists but Luke
quietly pointed out to me that my problem is that I keep
following up patients far longer than necessary,' Geoffrey
revealed. 'It was amazing to me that I'd never realised that
before. Now I'm trying to be less reluctant about referring
back to GPs. And I like what Luke's doing in Outpatients.
He's revolutionising the referral systems. In future our new
referrals are going to be pre-screened, which will cut down
enormously on follow-up appointments and waiting times.'

'Perhaps I'll look through one of my lists and see what
I come up with,' Annabel said reluctantly, Geoffrey's approval shaming her into the concession. 'But if I can't see
a straightforward way of cutting my numbers I'm going to
fight this. This is a hospital. We're not running a business
here. We can't be expected to put profits ahead of patients.'

Geoffrey looked a little taken aback by her vehemence.
'Annabel, before you do anything rash, talk to Luke,' he
advised seriously. 'Have him have an objective look at your
numbers.'

'*Objectionable*, more like.' But she managed a reluctant
smile in response to Geoffrey's sudden grin, pleased that
someone at least found the whole disastrous situation entertaining.

She checked her watch. 'I'd better get moving,' she told
him. They'd grabbed a coffee together at the canteen after
their respective ward rounds. 'That lady I told you about
after clinic on Monday—you remember, the Italian lady
with the atrial myxoma—is having her operation this morn-

ing. I want to pop up and say hello to her before she goes to theatre.'

Mrs Di Bella was sitting bolt upright in bed in one of the side cubicles on G ward, fully dressed in a tie-back cream theatre gown, cotton bootees and a frilled paper hat, her daughter and her daughter's fiancé holding one hand each. 'The nurse said the porters will be here any minute,' Mrs Di Bella told her when Annabel peeked in. 'They gave me an injection an hour ago. They said it would give me a dry mouth and make me feel calmer but it hasn't affected me at all. It's going to be all right, Dr Stuart. Please, tell me it's going to be all right.'

'You're going to be fine.' Annabel had been in to see her the afternoon before after her clinic and had done her best to reassure her, but she was clearly still very nervous. 'Perfectly fine. Hello, Carla. Gino.' She'd met both young people on a previous visit and now she strove for a normal atmosphere by looking away from her patient to greet them. 'I like your hair like that,' she told Carla, noticing the elaborate way she'd folded and twisted it up the long strands onto her head. 'It's lovely. That really suits you.'

'She's going to wear it like that for the wedding,' her patient told her tearfully. 'I told her I wanted to see it done properly just once.'

Carla leaned forward and patted her mother's arm above where she still clutched her other one. 'You'll see it at the wedding, Mama.'

'You'll come down with me to the theatre, Dr Stuart, won't you?' Mrs Di Bella released her future son-in-law's hand to clutch at Annabel's. 'That would give me more confidence. I think of you as my good luck charm. Will you come with me?'

'Of course.' Annabel agreed immediately despite her surprise at hearing herself described as a good luck charm.

Considering she'd been the one to make Mrs Di Bella's diagnosis, she would have thought the other woman would have considered her more the opposite. 'Just let me make one call to warn my clinic I'll be delayed,' she said gently. 'OK?'

Mrs Di Bella released her hand with reluctance and when Annabel hurried back a few seconds later she grabbed it again and held it tight. When the theatre porters eventually arrived, Annabel went with them, still holding her patient's hand as she was wheeled to the central bank of lifts and then to the main operating theatres.

Racing down to Outpatients after delivering Mrs Di Bella to the anaesthetist who'd be responsible for her care all the time she was in Theatres, Annabel almost cannoned into Luke as she dashed around the corner into the department. Only his arm, grabbing her and lifting her aside before she hit him, stopped a direct collision.

She looked up at him, breathless, an apology ready, but his disapproving green glare made it die on her lips before she could voice it. 'Where's the emergency?' he demanded.

'No emergency,' she answered hurriedly. 'I'm just running late—'

'Twenty-five minutes late for an already heavily over-booked clinic,' he pointed out coldly. 'Eighteen patients have been waiting more than thirty minutes. Your registrar's doing her best but she shouldn't be left to work unsupervised. I expect better of my staff, Annabel. If you can't cope with your workload, talk to me and I'll arrange to have it reduced to reasonable levels.'

'I don't have a problem with my workload,' she said through gritted teeth, furious that he'd been spying on her clinic and resenting his attitude. In all her time here Harry had never once complained about her clinics. She glared up at him fiercely. 'There's only one thing around here I have a problem with, and it's got a face like thunder and it's standing right in front of me.'

He didn't look amused. 'Get used to it,' he said grimly. 'I'm here to stay.'

Annabel turned to stare at his back as he stalked off, only just resisting the childish urge to poke out her tongue.

When she'd left Mrs Di Bella at Theatres, the older woman had been desperate that Annabel agree to be there with her *if* she ever made it out of the place. As soon as she got a spare second Annabel rang the surgical intensive care unit as all post-op open-heart surgery patients went to the unit routinely at least overnight. The unit's ward clerk cheerfully agreed to bleep her immediately her patient was transferred.

'Bit nervous, is she?' she asked brightly.

'Petrified,' Annabel agreed. 'Thanks, Valerie. I appreciate it.'

'Oop, better go and touch up my lipstick.' The ward clerk giggled. 'The new professor's just walked in to see one of our admissions and I wanted to be looking my most beautiful. Bye, Dr Stuart. Talk to you soon.'

'Bye, Valerie.' *Lipstick.* Annabel banged the receiver down in disgust. Was she the only woman in the whole hospital not running herself ragged trying to impress Luke?

She almost felt a small sense of triumph at that until, abruptly, she looked down at herself and flushed. The bright, summery dress she was wearing was one she'd taken out of a dry-cleaning bag that morning for the first time in years. While it reached the top of her knees and was not at all clinging or revealing, the silky, button-front frock was still far lighter and more youthful than anything she'd worn before Luke's criticism the night she'd gone to the movies with Geoffrey. Obviously, despite her smugness, she was, even more than Valerie, dressing to please "the new professor".

And any arguments with herself that the dress was simply more comfortable than one of her longer ones or a suit now that it seemed warmer weather had arrived to stay were irrelevant because part of her annoyance with Luke that morning had stemmed from a very definite feeling of pique that he hadn't noticed her outfit. Disgusted with herself for being so transparently pathetic, she vowed to go out of her way to wear something long and colourless the next day.

A little while later the absurdity of that, and of the way she was continuing to react to Luke, suddenly struck her. Geoffrey had been right that morning, she realised sadly. She was treating and reacting to Luke her ex-husband rather than Luke her new boss.

Next time there was a gap in her session, while the patient she needed to examine undressed, she fished in her desk and retrieved the latest classified advertisement section of *The Lancet*. She opened the journal to the section dealing with cardiology vacancies. She loved St Peter's, and until Luke's return she'd imagined seeing out the length of her career here. But perhaps now the sanest thing was to admit she wasn't going to be able to cope with him. And if she was leaving, it was best she went early. It was time to acknowledge defeat, sacrifice her job and go away quietly.

CHAPTER TEN

MRS DI BELLA arrived on the unit awake and breathing on her own, but extensively monitored. Annabel noted a line into her neck, recording her heart's function, along with cardiac leads, an indwelling arterial line plus several venous lines connected to pumps controlling her medications and fluids, a catheter into her bladder and a little tag on her ear connected to a machine that displayed her blood oxygen saturation levels.

'I am alive, Dr Stuart,' she rasped sleepily but triumphantly through her oxygen mask.

Annabel smiled. 'The operation went well.' Simon Rawlings, Mrs Di Bella's surgeon, had bleeped her at the end of the operation. 'He's removed all the tumour and patched up the hole it left in your heart wall.'

'Thank you, Dr Stuart.' Her patient's eyes started to droop shut. 'Thank you so much. My daughter...?'

'Carla will be allowed to come in a little later,' Annabel told her. 'You should sleep for a while now. I'll come back and see you tonight.'

Annabel stopped at the desk to thank Valerie again on her way out. 'She was very nervous pre-op,' she explained to the unit's charge nurse, who was standing with the ward clerk at the main desk. 'According to Simon, everything was straightforward.'

'She had a burst of A Fib when we were transferring her,' Catherine told her, referring to a type of disordered heart rhythm of the sort Mrs Di Bella had had intermittently prior to her admission. 'We called the registrar but she reverted back to sinus rhythm before he could get here. Her rhythm's been stable since.'

Annabel frowned. Mrs Di Bella had been taking a beta-blocker drug pre-operatively to try and prevent the disturbed rhythm, which wasn't uncommon in the first twenty-four hours after this sort of surgery. It was good that her rhythm had come back to normal without further treatment, but it was possible it might recur in future or might even become a permanent rhythm.

If it did, Annabel would need to prescribe blood thinners to reduce the risk of Mrs Di Bella having a stroke or arterial blockage as a result. She couldn't give her patient blood thinners yet because they would increase the risk of her haemorrhaging from her surgical wounds, and for the moment it was important for her simply to recover from her surgery.

'How's Daisy Miller?' Catherine asked. 'Tony mentioned she was back in again but she hasn't been up to see us here. He said she hasn't bounced back too well this admission.'

'She's a little better,' Annabel conceded. 'She can walk to the bathroom now, and with Daisy that means she's raring to go dancing again so I'll probably have to let her out. There's a fund-raising dinner tomorrow night, which she's been helping to arrange, and I suspect nothing short of a transplant turning up will stop her getting to it.'

'We heard her new boyfriend contributed some huge amount.'

'He's been great,' Annabel agreed with a smile. Daisy worked tirelessly at raising funds for cardiac research and it seemed her boyfriend had now been coaxed to help. 'Also, he organised his team-mates to sign football shirts to be auctioned. Daisy says they'll bring in a few pounds.'

'Hundreds, probably,' Daisy told her when Annabel

asked her about the shirts later that day on her evening ward
round. She fiddled with the adjustment of the oxygen tubing
behind her ears. 'Perhaps more since they're so near the
top of the league this year.'

'Is that uncomfortable?' Annabel moved behind her and
lifted the tubing slightly, checking to see there was no redness developing behind her ears. 'Want me to ask the
nurses to pad it for you or would you prefer to change to
a mask?'

'Padding might help,' Daisy answered. 'Thanks.'

Annabel sat on the edge of her bed, looked through her
results from that morning and her observation chart and
exchanged a carefully neutral look with Hannah, before
turning back to her patient. 'I was half expecting you to be
begging me to let you go home tonight.'

Daisy struggled up on the pillows behind her back and
head. 'Tomorrow's OK,' she said, her words confirming
Annabel's fears that she really wasn't feeling any better. 'I
want to be really well for the dinner. You're still coming,
aren't you, Dr Stuart?'

'If I'm not needed here,' Annabel confirmed. She'd
bought her ticket several weeks earlier and had arranged to
be seated at the same table as Harry and his wife and a
group of doctors and their partners from the paediatric side
of the hospital. 'Daisy, I'm worried about your blood oxygen readings. Your levels are still dropping too much
when we take you off the oxygen.'

'You think it's time for home oxygen.'

'As a trial to start,' Annabel admitted gently. The point
was more that Daisy wasn't well enough to leave St Peter's
without oxygen. In the past they'd discussed the possibility
of home oxygen therapy in an abstract way, but the time
had come to talk specifics. 'I'd like our technician to visit
your flat and arrange for it to start.'

'Not for twenty-four hours,' Daisy said huskily. 'Dr Stuart, I know you're only doing what's best for me but I couldn't bear—'

'When you're home in the evenings and mornings and overnight,' Annabel interrupted. The oxygen cylinder would be mounted on a trolley, allowing some degree of mobility, and for up to eight hours maximum per day she could be without it. 'If you're going out in the evenings you can compensate by wearing it for the same time during the day instead.'

'If it has to be, it has to be.' Daisy's tremulous smile just about broke Annabel's heart. 'I suppose at least that way I'll look pink and healthy for the dinner tomorrow. I won't have to worry about scaring off the paying guests.'

'You'd hardly do that,' Annabel said quietly. 'Half the people on the guest list are probably only coming to see you.'

'I may have been a teeny bit forceful in my invitations,' Daisy conceded gravely, although the twinkle was back in her eyes now. 'But it's for a good cause.'

'A very good one,' Annabel agreed.

Daisy smiled. 'That's a nice dress, Dr Stuart. I haven't seen you in anything as feminine as that before. It suits you. Will you be wearing something like that tomorrow night?'

Annabel, blinking a little at Daisy's abrupt change of subject, looked down at herself and smoothed a silky pleat over her knees. 'I haven't thought about it,' she admitted. People tended to dress fairly formally for these sorts of occasions and she had a couple of suitable outfits but she hadn't had time to consider which she'd wear yet.

'You should.' Daisy nodded. 'That style suits you.'

With Daisy's comment in mind, Annabel went to more effort than she would have usually for the dinner. She took a few hours off on Saturday afternoon and for the first time in more than a year she went clothes-shopping. The emerald sleeveless dress she eventually chose scooped at the neck into a narrow bodice and waist then flared in two pleats over her hips to just below her knees.

The neckline hadn't looked immodest in the store but it was lower than she was used to and she felt a little self-conscious, but a quick glance around the crowd when she arrived at the hotel soothed her anxiety that she might stand out because there were women in all sorts of outfits from short cocktail frocks to long, formal ballgowns.

She spotted Harry and his wife Evelyn at the far side of the foyer and began making her way slowly in their direction, smiling and nodding and exchanging greetings with familiar faces as she moved.

'Annabel, you look absolutely lovely.' Evelyn kissed her cheek when she reached them. 'You've bought a new dress. Harry, don't just stand there with your mouth open. Tell Annabel she looks lovely.'

'Always does,' Harry said gallantly, adjusting his bow-tie.

Annabel, flushing slightly, thanked them both and complimented Evelyn on her own beautiful dress. 'Quite a gathering, isn't it? I don't think I've ever seen such a good turn-out. I don't see too many people I recognise. Have you seen Daisy, Harry?'

'Looking radiant and clinging to her young man,' Harry told her with a chuckle.

Only Daisy could look radiant with a blood oxygen pressure as low as hers was, Annabel acknowledged ruefully. 'I might go and have a peek at her,' she told the couple. Because she'd known the occasion was so important to Daisy she hadn't had the heart to insist she spend the eve-

ning instead in her bed at St Peter's, but inwardly she
hadn't been relaxed about releasing her.

The crowd had gathered in the foyer and mezzanine level
of the hotel around the balconies, and there were only a
few couples in the ballroom on the first floor where the last
of the tables were still being set up by hotel staff. Annabel
spotted Daisy, sitting with her boyfriend at an otherwise
empty table at the far side of the hall. Their backs were to
her, but when she walked closer, wanting to get a closer
look at Daisy's skin colour, she felt an arm curl around
hers and she whirled around to confront Luke.

'Leave her,' he ordered quietly.

'Why?' She stared up at him, her senses reacting to the
devastating sight of her ex-husband in a dinner jacket. 'I
didn't know you were coming,' she added jerkily. 'Harry
never mentioned it. Where are you sitting? Not with us, I
shouldn't think. Our table's full.' Not giving him a chance
to answer, she tugged at his arm, wanting him to release
her. 'I have to see Daisy. Her blood oxygen level this afternoon was terrible—'

'Leave her for now,' Luke said more forcefully. 'Give
them space. I was checking the microphone over there a
few minutes ago and I think I overheard him getting ready
to propose.'

'*John?*' Annabel's mouth dried. She whirled quickly and
saw the couple still bent closely together then turned back
to Luke. 'Oh, the poor man,' she said faintly. 'He doesn't
realise she's dying.'

'Or perhaps he does,' Luke murmured.

Annabel felt tears prickle behind her eyes. She let her
evening bag slide off her shoulder and started to open it to
find a tissue, but Luke offered her a white handkerchief,
slid a warm arm around her back and guided her through
a side door into a deserted hotel corridor.

'Thanks.' Annabel dabbed her eyes and drew in a shuddering breath. 'Actually, I don't know how much she's told him,' she said weakly. 'Probably, knowing Daisy, not much. He knows she's waiting for a transplant, of course, but I doubt if he understands how urgently she needs it.'

'It might not change anything if he does.' Luke rubbed the pad of his thumb across her moist cheek. 'He's in love. He wants to be with her every minute he still can be.'

'That's curiously romantic, coming from you.' Annabel wiped her cheek again where he'd touched her, but this time with his handkerchief. 'How do you know about feelings like that?'

He took the handkerchief out of her hands and rubbed gently at a space she must have missed. 'Is it so inconceivable I could have felt that way about you?'

'You never wanted to be with me every minute. You wanted an hour, now and then, for sex, but outside that you wouldn't have cared.'

'They were demanding years,' he countered. 'For both of us. There were times when I wanted you and you weren't there for me either. Times when you slept at the hospital rather than come home to me.'

'The difference is that I'd have come if you'd asked.' Her tears dried now, she rested back against the cool wall of the corridor and closed her eyes. 'I would have done anything for you.'

'Liar.' His face was bleak. 'I asked you to come to Boston.'

'That old thing.' Annabel lowered her head. 'You'll simmer about that for ever won't you? Well, you shouldn't have tried to bully me. If you'd asked me nicely I'd have gone to the moon with you, Luke. And if the job was that important to you, why didn't you just leave me then and go right away when they first asked you?'

'You were my wife,' he said flatly, as if that was all the answer she needed. 'You're not seriously saying you didn't come because I didn't put it to you politely enough? Annabel, you knew how important that position was to me.'

'I wanted to be more important.'

'You *were* more important. I stayed, didn't I?'

'Reluctantly and resentfully.'

'There were things I wanted to achieve in my professional life,' he said grimly. 'Until you, I'd worked hard and single-mindedly for them. I didn't expect to have to delay that progress and, you're right, I did find that frustrating. But when I'd least wanted to I'd fallen in love, and more than anything else in the world I wanted to make you happy. I'm sorry that I didn't find it as easy to put aside my professional aspirations as I should have. I'm sorry that you and our marriage suffered for my ambivalence, but in the end I did what I thought was right.'

'By which you mean, put the job on hold temporarily, hang around until life gets tedious, then dump me and make a quick escape,' she summarised. 'Thanks very much, Luke. You did me a real favour.'

'The greatest favour I did you was leaving. You were a gifted, talented doctor and suddenly you were talking about leaving hospital medicine for general practice or even giving up altogether,' he said accusingly. 'If I'd stayed you'd have thrown away your career.'

'To have your child.'

'We had years ahead of us for children,' he said dismissively. 'You've still time ahead of you now if you wanted to delay. There was never any rush. And you love your job, don't you? When I asked you about regrets this week you admitted you had none.'

'You're trying to judge me by your own standards but they don't apply to me,' she protested. 'If what you want is belated thanks for rescuing me from a life of tedious domesticity, Luke, then I'm sorry—you're out of luck. I do love my job, I adore it, but I'd have found a little part-time general practice, combined with raising children, just as, if not more, rewarding. I never wanted "the big career".' She put the last three words in quotes by wiggling her fingers in the air. 'You're the only one who rated your career more important than a family or me.'

Luke's gaze narrowed down to her face. 'You just can't leave it alone, can you, Annie? It's impossible to have a conversation, without you bringing my failings back into it somewhere. Why did you have to see my work as competition to you?'

'Because I was *sick* with jealousy,' she said baldly, glaring up at him. '*Sick* with it. I wanted you just once to want me as much as you wanted to get ahead in your job.' She averted her eyes from his suddenly thoughtful expression and turned away from him. 'We'd better go back. I can hear people gathering.'

Annabel looked for Daisy as she made her way to where she could see Harry and his wife already seated at their table, but the younger woman didn't seem to be about anywhere, although she tapped Annabel on her shoulder a few minutes later at the table as people were beginning to settle into their seats.

'The dress is perfect, Dr Stuart. You look amazing.'

'How are you feeling?' Annabel looked up searchingly. Behind Daisy's smile her face was pale and her eyes red, and John, standing behind her, looked tense and strained, his eyes, too, suspiciously swollen.

'Oh, you can forget me. You're not at work now.' She bent and spoke close to Annabel's ear. 'I've got a surprise for you,' she murmured. 'I organised the tables and guess which gorgeous professor's going to be sitting next to you tonight? You will make the most of it, won't you, Dr Stuart? I really think he likes you.'

Annabel looked up. Luke had been waylaid, after returning to the room, by one of Daisy's fellow fund-raising committee members, but the chair next to hers was the only conspicuously vacant one she could see now in the entire room. 'Daisy,' she warned, 'don't even begin to waste your time thinking about it.'

'I asked him,' Daisy whispered. 'He's not married. He isn't even seeing anyone at the moment.'

'You're a menace,' Annabel said weakly.

'Be nice to him just for me.' Dimpling, Daisy put her hand into the crook of John's elbow and the couple moved away towards the next table.

There was a flurry of greetings when Luke reached the table, and Annabel realised from Harry's bland welcome that she was probably the only one who hadn't been expecting him.

Buying a book of raffle tickets from one of the circulating sellers took a few minutes, then she turned to Harry beside her. Luke was occupied in conversation with doctors she recognised from the Harefield Hospital, a specialist heart and chest hospital in Middlesex, who'd come up to introduce themselves to him. 'I thought Martin Briggs was going to be here,' she whispered to Harry. The senior paediatric cardiologist at St Peter's, the man she'd expected to find herself seated next to, had been scheduled as the star after-dinner speaker for the evening.

'Came down with viral vestibulitis on Wednesday,' Harry explained, referring to an ear condition which could cause dramatic dizziness. 'Young Daisy Miller immediately invited Luke and happily he agreed to step in and speak at the last minute.' Harry beamed. He patted his stomach in a satisfied way. 'Sold another dozen tables in half a day

once word got around,' he said smugly. 'That's why we're
in the ballroom instead of down in the restaurant. There're
even journalists here tonight. We might get some good pub-
licity out of this.'

Their first courses were delivered during a brief welcoming speech by the master of ceremonies for the evening,
one of the medical scientists from St Peter's. There were
two choices, delivered alternately around the table, and despite her tenseness at Luke's proximity Annabel enjoyed
her asparagus. When the main courses were delivered she
was given steak with a wild mushroom sauce, but before
she could decide what she was going to do about that Luke,
still deep in discussion with the paediatrician on his other
side, smoothly and wordlessly swapped her meal for his
poached salmon.

'I've never understood why you ladies prefer fish to
meat,' Harry pronounced, beaming at Annabel, having just
performed a similar meal swap with his wife. 'Can you not
see, Annabel, that there's no greater culinary treat than a
nicely cooked piece of Scottish beef like this?'

'I'm sure it's lovely but if I eat mushrooms I'm risking
anaphylaxis,' Annabel explained. 'I'm allergic to them,'
she added quickly, seeing Evelyn's puzzlement at the medical term. 'My face and neck swell up and I get wheezy
and covered in a rash. I've been like that since childhood.
It's years since I've tried a mushroom but I won't ever be
brave enough to go near one again.'

A short time later Luke concluded his conversation with
the paediatrician and turned back to her. 'All right?'

'It's very nice.' Annabel cut herself another tiny piece
of the delicately flavoured fish. 'Thank you for that, although after all this time I'm surprised you still remembered.'

He smiled. 'The sight of you swelling up like a puffer fish isn't something I'm ever likely to forget.'

Annabel flushed. 'I imagine I must have looked pretty repulsive,' she murmured, lowering her eyes. She'd pursued him to one of the hospital's cafés one day a couple of months into her very earliest infatuation with him but, instead of impressing him with witty lunch-hour conversation, she'd been so flustered she'd inadvertently eaten several mushrooms in a salad. Luke had had to drag her off to Casualty for a shot of antihistamine.

'I wasn't worried about what you looked like,' he said roughly. 'I thought you were going to go into shock on me, Annie. I'd never seen anyone react so fast before.'

'You were annoyed with me for being such a nuisance,' she recalled.

'I wasn't annoyed, I was cold with fear.' He looked impatient. 'I had visions of having to ruin that beautiful neck of yours by cutting a tracheostomy with a pair of plastic cafeteria knives.'

Annabel lifted an involuntary hand to her throat. 'It's just an ordinary neck,' she said faintly.

He sent her a terse look. 'Eat your salmon. You've barely touched it and it'll be getting cold.'

After the sweet course the doctor in charge of proceedings rose again and spoke for a short while about the aims and achievements of the foundation, then began Luke's introduction by saying he was sure he had no need for one. Nevertheless, he proceeded to give him a lengthy, hugely enthusiastic one, and Annabel joined in the applause as Luke walked from the table to the microphone-equipped lectern next to the main table.

Luke thanked the older doctor for his generosity and the audience for theirs. But then, instead of the intellectual discourse about heart disease or a discussion of the research work for which he'd been tipped to win a Nobel Prize the previous year which Annabel half expected, Luke, clearly an accomplished after-dinner speaker, gave a talk that appealed to his audience as a whole, lay people as well as medical members, rather than one tailored to his fellow doctors.

For around forty minutes, while they drank their after-dinner coffee and port, he related an entertaining mix of anecdotes about differences he'd encountered between hospitals and life in general in England and the US and the difficulties he was now experiencing, trying to fit back into English life after six years in the country of his birth.

Annabel found herself frequently joining in the laughter that greeted his stories, and she was pleased to see that Daisy and John, too, seemed to be enjoying the speech, but she, along with the rest of the audience, sobered quickly once Luke moved seamlessly onto the more serious side of his talk, medical research and the sort of work to which the funds they contributed that evening would be put.

'Cardiac disease accounts for around half of all deaths in this country,' he concluded. 'Even small advances have the potential to prevent enormous premature loss of life. Please, give generously.'

After the applause the master of ceremonies returned to the lectern beside Luke to field questions. There were dozens about Luke's research and about whether he'd be continuing similar work at St Peter's, to which he said yes, and that a guarantee of expanded funding for his work had been part of the reason he'd returned. Then a woman at the table next to Annabel's asked about his reasons for entering the field he had and also about what the trigger had been for his decision to return to London and St Peter's.

'Surprisingly, perhaps, my answers to both questions are closely linked,' Luke said slowly. 'Returning to St Peter's is like coming full circle for me. In many ways I feel very much as if it's where I belong in the world. I spent a year at the hospital as a registrar, but the most significant contact I had with it occurred two days after my ninth birthday when my brother died on the paediatric intensive care unit of heart failure secondary to a viral heart infection.'

Annabel turned cold. The stark hush that followed his words was immediately different to the good-humoured mood of the audience throughout the rest of his talk.

'Justin was only eleven but his disease had been rapidly progressive,' Luke told them quietly. 'He died quietly and courageously within three months of the start of his illness. I knew then that I wanted to do something with my life that might make a difference, something that might one day stop another family having to go through what we went through that year.

'I and my colleagues in the field are still trying to do that. We don't have a cure for cardiomyopathy and our treatments remain limited, but with your help and support we may get a little further along the path. Thank you for your generosity in coming tonight, ladies and gentlemen, and thank you for your generosity in listening.'

There was a brief pause followed by a burst of applause which Luke acknowledged by lifting his hand as he came back to his seat beside Annabel who was still concentrating fiercely on preventing herself crying again.

She had known his only brother had died in childhood because Luke's mother had mentioned it once in passing. But she hadn't known how exactly or when or what his disease had been or the significance of it, and at the time she'd felt she hadn't known Luke's mother well enough to have questioned her further. Luke had changed the subject abruptly the only time she'd ever tried to talk to him about it.

As the applause abated, the chairman thanked Luke solemnly for sharing his experiences with them, then moved on to what he termed the 'business' end of the evening—the auction, the depositing of written pledges into the circulating buckets and the drawing of the raffles they'd all bought tickets for earlier.

Annabel sat through all of it in a daze, for once barely aware even of Luke although, turned as they all were in their seats to face the auctioneer, he was directly behind her.

Afterwards there was to be dancing but when the music started and the first couples began emerging onto the cleared floor she turned back towards the table and felt Luke's eyes on her immediately. 'Dance with me, Annie?'

'Perhaps later,' she said softly. 'I'm on call. I have to go and check the hospital.' Sitting next to her the way he was, she understood that it would be natural for him to ask her, that the others at the table might even be surprised if he didn't, but right then she was feeling too emotional. The last thing she could cope with was trying to maintain a front of social casualness while being held in his arms in public. Avoiding looking at him, she excused herself from the table.

'Nothing much happening on our side at all,' Hannah told her when she called St Peter's and had the registrar bleeped. 'By the looks of it so far, we've picked a great weekend to be on call. Mark and I have been in the mess most of the night, eating pizza and watching telly, and I haven't had any calls about possible admissions. The surgeons must be busy, though, because we saw a couple of the registrars running down the main corridor a little while ago, but I haven't heard what that's about yet. How's Daisy doing?'

'Coping,' Annabel told her, knowing the younger doctor

had shared her concern about allowing her out so early. 'Just. Her colour isn't good and I was worried when she didn't eat anything but she and John were first up on the dance floor.'

'That's young love for you,' Hannah said.

Annabel felt wistful. 'Let me know if anything comes in,' she told the younger doctor. 'I'm leaving now so I should be on my home number in about twenty minutes.'

Her bleeper sounded just as she was letting herself into the house, but before she could answer it her telephone rang anyway. 'Hello,' she said breathlessly, picking it up quickly as there was only one person who could be calling her at this hour. 'What is it, Hannah?'

However, it wasn't her registrar but Tony Grant who answered her. 'We've got a heart,' he told her rapidly. 'We're still going through final testing but it's looking like a possible match for Daisy Miller.'

CHAPTER ELEVEN

'I'VE bleeped Daisy to come in now,' Tony continued, 'along with one other potential recipient with the same blood group. Theatre's scheduled at this stage for one-thirty.'

Annabel's watch read eleven-thirty. 'I'll be there in fifteen minutes,' she decided quickly. Her role, if she were needed, would be purely advisory, but she preferred to be on site.

Hannah meet her on J ward. 'You look nice, Dr Stuart. Daisy's upstairs,' she told Annabel. 'Professor Geddes drove her from the dinner. John's with her and her aunt's on her way in. Mr Grant thinks she's going to be the closest match.'

Annabel's heart had leapt at the mention of Luke's name but she told herself he'd be long gone now. She made a dismissive gesture towards her dress. She'd grabbed a white coat from the ward but she hadn't taken time to change into casual clothes. 'Who's the other woman?' she asked as they headed for the stairs.

Hannah told her the name and she nodded. Annabel knew her but she wasn't one of her patients.

'Is Daisy OK?'

Hannah grimaced. 'Scared,' she said flatly.

Annabel saw what Hannah meant as soon as she saw Daisy. The younger woman smiled at them but behind her oxygen mask her face was white and tense. She was sitting bolt upright in bed, wearing a white cotton theatre gown which she'd forgotten to tie behind her.

'John's just gone to ring his parents,' she told them huskily. 'I said there's no point because there's no way of knowing yet, but he wanted to let them know anyway. Dr Stuart, I feel sick.'

'It's normal to be nervous,' Annabel said soothingly. She also felt sick. She went behind Daisy and gently knotted the ties of her gown. 'Have they been to take blood yet?'

'About ten gallons of it,' Daisy answered. 'And I've had another chest X-ray and an ECG. I'm not allowed to have anything to eat or drink and they've given me a tablet to make my stomach empty. When do you think they'll know?'

'Mr Grant will come and see you as soon as he hears anything.'

'What about the person who died?' asked Daisy. 'Was it an accident? Do you know what happened to them?'

Annabel shook her head. She tucked one of Daisy's blonde ringlets back behind her ear from where it had fallen across her oxygen mask. 'I haven't heard.' If the family of donors agreed, the recipient could find out details about the donor and even meet the family, but she knew nothing yet.

'The dinner was good, wasn't it?' Daisy sent her a wan look. 'We raised a lot of money. I was waiting for you to dance with Professor Geddes but you left and you didn't come back.'

'I was tired.' Annabel looked up as John appeared at the door to the room with a cup of coffee. 'Hannah and I will go and see if we can find your ECG and X-ray,' she told Daisy. 'We'll be back in a little while.'

She hesitated when she saw Luke, still in formal dress, at the main desk, talking with Tony Grant. Ignoring Hannah's appreciative sigh and the way the registrar looked on the verge of swooning beside her, she took a deep breath and made her slightly wobbly way—she still wasn't used to wearing heels again yet and her nervousness made walking more difficult—towards them again. 'Any news, Tony?'

'Not yet.' The surgeon turned towards her, blinked, then grinned. 'Wow!'

Annabel felt herself colour. Her hands fumbling, she gathered her white coat around her and buttoned it firmly. 'I was at a fund-raising dinner tonight.'

'So Luke was just saying.'

'Thank you for driving Daisy and John back,' Annabel said huskily, lifting her eyes to her ex-husband. 'That was kind of you.'

'My dance partner had vanished and John looked so nervous there seemed a fair chance he'd crash the bike,' Luke said neutrally. 'We looked around for you but you were nowhere in sight. Where did you disappear off to so fast? If you were scared about dancing with me, Annie, you only had to say no. I couldn't have forced you. Not in public.'

Annabel's flush deepened hotly. Both Tony and Hannah, looking startled, suddenly developed urgent things needing their attention and the pair melted away, leaving Annabel facing Luke on her own.

'Thanks,' she said weakly. 'That's really great, Luke. Great. Now I'll have to put up with Hannah's curious little looks for the next month while she ponders whether we're having some secret affair. And that's just exactly what I need. I went home. Is that good enough for you? I was tired and I went home.'

'Without telling anyone?' he remarked doubtfully.

'The dinner was virtually finished—'

'You used to enjoy dancing with me.'

But the way dancing with Luke had once made her feel was exactly the reason she'd been so afraid of him tonight. 'That was a long time ago.'

'Frightened I'd step on your toes?'

'Terrified,' she agreed. 'If that's Daisy's X-ray you're holding, may I see it, please?'

Wordlessly he slid the film out of its blue envelope and snapped it up onto the X-ray board beside the desk, staying silent while she inspected it.

'Have you seen her ECG around anywhere?'

'One of the anaesthetic registrars has it. I was here so I had a look at it when it was done and there was no change.'

'Thank you.' Annabel fastened then undid the top button on her coat, then bit her lower lip and looked at him. 'I… Luke, I'm sorry about your brother. I didn't realise how he died.'

'It was a long time ago.'

'Nevertheless, I'm sorry I never understood. I'd always assumed there was some…selfishness in your pursuit of your career, and tonight for the first time I realised that I was the selfish one. Your research work in Boston could be the start of something that will eventually help thousands of people. If you'd gone two years earlier when they first invited you, perhaps by now—'

'The date I went was irrelevant,' he told her quietly. 'We worked as a team there. What we achieved was a reflection of that teamwork, not of my own achievements. Temporarily I was in charge of the project and that meant I was given credit for what we achieved, but the work started before I was there and it's still ongoing.'

Annabel lowered her head. It was kind of him to tell her that but she didn't believe the timing of his arrival at the university had been so inconsequential. The thought that she'd been so tied up with her own petty grievances about how much time he'd allocated to her to even consider the importance of his work filled her with self-disgust.

Two of the nurses who'd been at the other end of the ward, checking their sleeping patients, came quietly up the ward towards them. 'Any news yet on which one of them's for the transplant?' asked one.

Annabel shook her head. 'Tony Grant's going to call as soon as he knows,' she told them. She looked quickly at Luke, then hastily back down at her watch. 'It's after midnight,' she said huskily. 'I'll check Daisy again and then I'll be waiting in my office. Goodnight, everyone.'

She'd assumed either the ward or Hannah would bleep her directly once a decision had been made about the transplant, but instead Luke came to her office a short while later. 'Daisy's the best match. They're taking her in ten minutes.'

'I'll come down.' Annabel had been too nervous to get any work done, and now she shoved her paperwork away, grabbed her coat and hurried towards him.

There wasn't much time. She spent a few minutes with Daisy, who was pale and trembling, before one of the anaesthetic registrars arrived with the theatre porters to take her away. John went with her but Annabel stayed behind to reassure Caroline, Daisy's aunt, who'd just arrived and was looking tense and anxious.

When one of Caroline's friends arrived to sit with her Annabel left them alone, promising to return immediately when she heard any news. To her surprise Luke was on the ward. Still in his dinner jacket, he was studying a chest X-ray on the board near the darkened nursing station when she approached. 'Who's that?' she asked, puzzled by the dramatic lung changes on the film.

'Mr Lockett in side room four,' he told her quietly, sounding distracted. 'A man I admitted on Tuesday with chest pain who was coughing up blood. He's got staph endocarditis on his tricuspid valve. We had managed to get his temperature under control but it spiked twice again tonight.'

Annabel frowned. Endocarditis meant inflammation of the heart valves and staph indicated that that particular type of bacteria was actually growing on the valve, in this case the tricuspid valve on the right side of the heart. Although the changes in the man's lungs, caused by material thrown off from the heart valve, looked dramatic, the condition wasn't as serious as other types of endocarditis, which were often fatal, but it was seen particularly in intravenous drug users.

Addicts were vulnerable both because of their general poor physical state and lowered immunity and because the contaminates like starch and powders and sugars in heroin could damage heart valves and leave the users susceptible to infection.

'Is he in withdrawal?'

Luke shook his head. 'We're maintaining him on methadone,' he admitted. 'He's sick enough, without having to go through detox.'

Annabel nodded. Maintaining addicts was not strictly accepted protocol at St Peter's but she agreed with him in this case. 'Hannah and I will see him, Luke. You're not on call. Go home. I'll ECHO him to check his heart.'

'I just did it,' he said absently. 'His valve hasn't changed in two days. Your SHO's taken blood for culturing and he's changing his lines now in case they've become contaminated. We'll wait and watch with him overnight. You don't need to see him, Annabel. He's under control now. The ward will call me if there are problems.'

Considering the way he'd practically forced her out of the hospital the night he'd admitted Daisy, when he'd been on call, she found his insistence now on looking after his own patients hypocritical, but she knew there was little point in arguing with him. 'Have it your way,' she agreed wearily. 'I'm going back to my office.'

He looked up. 'Not home?'

'I wouldn't sleep, worrying about Daisy.' There was a glassed-in viewing and teaching room above the transplant theatre so she could look in on the procedure if she wanted, but when the surgery was being performed on her own patients she invariably found the process too nerve-racking to watch. 'If I'm going to be up all night anyway I may as well use the time usefully to get some paperwork done.'

'It's too late. You won't be able to concentrate.' Luke studied her steadily for long enough to make her feel nervous, then seemed to make up his mind about something. He put the X-ray away, then came towards her, took her elbow and turned her around. 'Come on. Let's go. You still owe me a dance.'

Annabel's mouth dried. 'I'm not going back to the dinner,' she protested, but she let him propel her out of the ward to the lifts. 'Even if it isn't finished it's too far away. I want to be here for when Tony bleeps me. And what if Hannah needs me?'

'She can bleep you,' he murmured. 'I'm not taking you far.'

'I shouldn't be letting you take me anywhere at all,' she said quietly, but she was weak and she loved him so she let him propel her down and out of the side door of the hospital into the car park and towards the expensive-looking dark sedan parked in the CEO's spot just outside. 'Is this yours?'

He shook his head but didn't explain, and she was left to draw her own conclusions from the yellow rental-car sticker on the rear window as she swung herself into the luxurious and new-smelling interior.

He waited quietly for her to settle herself then closed the passenger door. Annabel trembled as she watched him walk around the front of the car to his side.

His hotel was only a short distance from the hospital and most of the time was taken up waiting for a green light to turn out of the car park. If she needed to, she calculated, she'd be able to run back in less than five minutes.

She'd taken her white coat off in the car and folded it over her arm, but the knowing smile followed by the carefully bland expression of the hotel doorman's gaze as he opened the car door for her and looked at Luke made her flush and wish she'd kept her coat on. The assessing sideways look the receptionist sent her when Luke approached the desk came as confirmation of what the hotel staff probably thought.

Given the lateness of the hour and the fact that they must be used to Luke normally arriving alone, Annabel couldn't exactly blame them, but still she was offended and she glared back at the woman.

The amused look Luke sent her as they walked into the lift he'd summoned a few seconds later told her he'd noted her expression. 'In that dress you'd have to be a very high-class one,' he observed mildly. 'You look beautiful tonight, Annie. I could almost believe you're your old self again.'

'I'm only going to your room to leave my coat,' she warned huskily, flushing again. 'Then it's one dance at the nightclub and I'm leaving again straight away.'

'Is there a nightclub here?'

'Well, I assumed...' Annabel blinked. 'Isn't there?'

'Not that I know of.'

'Oh.' She lowered her eyes, her thoughts churning. She should be protesting, she knew. She should be angry with him for tricking her into coming with him, because he *had* tricked her. Only she wasn't. She wasn't angry at all. She was just...nervous. When the lift stopped and the doors opened she walked out mechanically, her heels sinking into

the thickly carpeted floor along the corridor as she allowed
his outstretched arm to guide her to the door at the end.

She saw she'd been wrong to assume he'd called at
Reception to collect a key because what he actually pro-
duced was a plastic strip resembling a credit card, and when
he slid it through a groove beside the door a green light
came on and the door clicked open.

She walked in quietly and looked around. To her relief,
instead of being confronted immediately with a bed, she
found herself in a sitting room with three armchairs, a mod-
erately large table with a set of upholstered seats and a wide
desk near the window which was strewn with paperwork
and journals, suggesting Luke spent a considerable amount
of his time there working. Through a door on the left she
glimpsed the bedroom and further through she could see
lights reflecting off what looked like marble tiles in his
bathroom.

He moved the table and chairs away from the centre of
the room and against the wall. 'Room to dance,' he explained when she sent him a questioning look. He smiled.
'Shame on you, Annie. Did you think I'd brought you here
to seduce you?'

Annabel's face turned hot again immediately but thankfully a discreet tap at the door saved her from needing to
come up with an answer.

The door was ajar, and in response to Luke's command
it swung open to reveal a waiter, bearing a portable sound
system and a selection of mini-discs. He connected the
equipment, inserted the disc Luke chose and withdrew with
a smile of thanks for the note Luke had smoothly passed
him, closing the door behind him.

Luke came to her and drew her unresisting body into his
arms, held one of her hands and slid his other low around
her hips as the low strains of one of her favourite jazz artists

swelled sleepily out of the system's small speakers. 'You're trembling,' he murmured against her ear. 'Are you still frightened for Daisy?'

'A little, but there's nothing I can do for her now,' she admitted. 'Mostly I'm terrified of you. I know you didn't bring me here just for a dance, Luke.'

'Don't you think you have a say in what happens?'

'I know I don't.' She laid her face against his chest and breathed in the warm, clean, Luke scent of him, dizzy with longing for him. 'But I couldn't bear it if it's because you feel sorry for me.'

'It's never been that, Annie.' His arms tightened around her. 'You must know it isn't that.'

'But you don't really want me—'

'You're not that stupid,' he said huskily. 'I've never stopped wanting you.' She felt the vibration of him lowering the zipper of her dress and the soft loosening at her bodice as he started to draw the fabric firmly away. 'Are you going to stop me this time?'

Stop him? She knew she should but she also knew she couldn't. 'No.'

'I'm glad.' The twist of his mouth frankly sensual, Luke lowered his head and captured her mouth, his hands sliding intimately from her shoulders to her thighs as he dispensed with her dress. When he lifted his head she was breathing as hard as he was and she felt her skin stain hot red as his eyes lowered to the silk covering her breasts and lower abdomen and then lifted to her face again.

'They're new,' she said faintly. 'I bought them today.'

He brought one hand up and outlined the scalloped lace edge of her bra, the soft, slow movement of his fingers against her skin making her tighten in his arms. 'Because you wanted me to see you like this?'

'I don't know.' She dropped her eyes, mesmerised by the

movement of his hand as it slid deliberately inside one cup and held her. She gasped. 'Perhaps.'

The ground shifted beneath her then disappeared as he lifted her into his arms and carried her into his bedroom and to his bed. He put her down then shrugged out of his jacket and came after her. She couldn't stop shaking. She was embarrassed in case he noticed but he just smiled and kissed her again.

Unhurriedly, as if she were a doll he was playing with, he rolled her over, unclipped the fastening of her bra and brought her back around, but when he brought his hand up to cup her again she saw his hand was trembling as much as hers and her doubts evaporated.

'I've missed you so much,' she whispered. She lifted her fingers and struggled clumsily with the fastenings of his shirt. 'I'm so nervous I can't stop shaking. You missed me too, a little bit, didn't you, Luke? You wouldn't be like this if you hadn't missed me.'

'I missed you,' he confirmed thickly, lowering his mouth to hers again with a murmur of approval when she parted her lips urgently. 'I missed you like crazy.'

Annabel wanted him, wanted everything, wanted everything to be perfect the way it had always been perfect, but it had been years and she was out of practice. She couldn't get his shirt undone and he had to help her, and then she fumbled awkwardly with his belt, her fingers impatient but stiff, and in the end he rolled off the bed and stripped off his own clothes quickly then came back to her and gathered her in his arms again.

Despite the care he took with his caresses, she couldn't stop feeling tense for he was big and her body had grown tight again over the years. When his hands slid beneath her buttocks and he entered her she stiffened and cried out.

Luke stilled immediately, his features strained and harsh. 'Annie…?'

Annabel squeezed her eyes shut, trying to block out the discomfort and her own embarrassment. 'Finish it,' she whispered. 'Please, just finish. I'll be all right.'

'You'll be *all right*?'

She could feel he was trying to be gentle but she felt stretched and uncomfortable. The pain of him withdrawing was almost as bad as his entrance, and she gasped again.

Luke rolled away from her and off the bed. '*All right?*' he repeated strongly. 'What the hell does that mean?'

'Don't.' Annabel hauled the far side of the quilt miserably over her naked body, rolled over and buried her face in the pillows. 'I'm sorry.' Her voice came out muffled. 'I didn't mean to put you off. It's just…it's been a long time for me.'

'Annie, I'm not criticising you.' His voice softened. She felt the dip in the bed as he knelt beside her, and through the thickness of the quilt she felt him stroke her back. 'It's not supposed to be *all right*,' he murmured. 'It's supposed to be great. I didn't want you to do this for me. I want you to want it, too.'

She peeked out of the quilt, meaning to explain that she had, that she still wanted him, that if he could just bear to try again she thought they'd be able to work through her discomfort, but the sound of her bleeper from her coat in the other room sent him moving to get it for her.

Annabel struggled around and was sitting up, wide-eyed and still encased in her quilt, when he came back. 'If it's about Daisy already it must be bad news,' she said apprehensively. 'They could have only just begun.'

'It looks more like an X-ray number than one from Theatres.' Luke checked the illuminated numerals along the top of her bleeper then indicated the telephone beside the bed. 'You'll have to dial one for an outside line then go through the hospital's switchboard.'

Hannah, sounding flustered, answered quickly. 'Dr Stuart, it's me,' she said in a rush. 'Don't worry, it's not Daisy. Last I heard from Theatres, her operation's going well.'

Annabel, feeling herself relaxing, shook her head quickly at Luke to reassure him about Daisy. 'What is it, Hannah?'

'One of Dr Solomon's post-heart-attack patients has gone into second-degree heart block and his heart rate's dropped to forty,' the registrar told her, referring to a problem where the heart's normal electrical conducting system was disrupted. 'I'm sorry to bother you about something so trivial but neither Mark nor I can get the pacing wire positioned properly. I've been trying almost an hour. I wondered if you could come in and take over for me?'

'I'll be there in ten minutes,' Annabel agreed. 'Where are you?'

'The first side room in main X-Ray,' the younger doctor told her. 'We'll be waiting. Thanks a lot.'

'I'll drive you.' Luke, obviously having grasped some of the urgency of the situation from her side of the conversation, reached for the telephone as soon as she set it down. 'Get dressed. I'll have the car brought around.'

'She said Daisy's doing fine.' Still clutching the quilt around her, Annabel slid off the bed, grabbed her bra and underwear from the floor where Luke had thrown them and hurried into the other room to get her dress. 'Luke, I can walk—' But he was already talking to someone on the telephone so she broke off and quickly dressed, then pulled on her white coat.

He emerged from the bedroom seconds later, looking calm and coolly athletic in sports-style pants, trainers and a grey sweatshirt. He opened the door and gestured for her to go ahead of him.

Annabel felt flushed and dishevelled and she avoided his eyes. Neither of them said anything on the way downstairs but once they were in the car and heading for the hospital she sent him a brief, guarded look. 'Luke…?' She clenched her fists in her lap. 'I think it's best we just forget—'

'Don't you dare, Annie.' He kept his eyes on the road but his words were impatient. 'Don't you *dare* tell me to forget tonight and start again tomorrow. You must know by now that never works.'

'Fine.' Annabel lowered her head, feeling sick because, of course that had been exactly what she'd been about to say. What she wanted was to try and forget tonight so they could start again another time afresh, but obviously he wasn't going to be able to put her abysmal performance out of his mind. Clearly, his desire for her had been temporary and not strong enough to survive the embarrassing mess she'd just made of everything. 'Just fine,' she said thickly.

He turned into the hospital's side car park and drove towards the entrance nearest X-Ray. She fumbled for the doorhandle, finally managing to wrench it open. 'But you'll find that remembering everything and brooding about them every hour of the day doesn't make them go away either,' she told him stiffly. 'Trust me, I've had years of experience.' Not waiting for his response to that, she jumped out awkwardly, slammed the door shut and ran inside.

CHAPTER TWELVE

DAISY went straight from Theatres to one of the transplant unit's intensive care beds. She was ventilated overnight and for most of the next day, but when Annabel returned the next evening to see her she was conscious and awake and she even managed a smile.

'Sore,' she rasped in response to Annabel's questions. 'And still a bit tired and woozy from all this pain stuff they're giving me, but otherwise great. I can breathe properly.' She took a breath to demonstrate and held up her hands. 'And, look, my hands are bright pink. I can't stop looking at them. I just can't believe the colour. Mr Grant says I'll be here another day but then I might be able to go to his normal ward.'

'You're doing very well,' Annabel agreed. Daisy was still on oxygen and would continue to be on it for the routine twenty-four hours post-operatively, but her colour and blood levels were better than they'd ever been in all the years Annabel had been treating her, which suggested the new heart was functioning perfectly. 'Well done.'

'John's been on the phone today to travel agents about our holiday.' Daisy lifted her arms in a victorious way. 'He's finding out the best way to ship his Harley. Look out, Australia,' she declared huskily. 'Here we come.'

Annabel laughed. Life wasn't going to always be easy for Daisy from now on because for the rest of her life she'd have to take strong medication to try and prevent her immune system from rejecting her new heart. Particularly in the first few months she'd be vulnerable to infections as well since the high doses of the drugs she'd be taking would render her immune system very weak. Also, she'd have frequent heart biopsies, weekly at first, to monitor her for signs of rejection. But predictably, it seemed, she wasn't about to let little hurdles like that slow her down.

'And thanks, Dr Stuart.' Daisy dimpled at her. 'For everything, I mean. All these years. Thank you.'

'You're very welcome.' Annabel felt tearful suddenly. 'I'll be back to see you in the morning, Daisy. Sleep well.'

She checked with Hannah to make sure there was no one she needed to see, then headed home.

After her weekend on call and the dramatic events of the night before she should have slept well but, of course, she didn't.

She didn't see Luke at all Monday and although she'd inwardly steeled herself for encountering him at the Dean's lecture on Tuesday he wasn't there, and Harry arrived to introduce the session instead. On Wednesday she heard from the nurses in clinic that Luke was away until Friday at some conference which had been set up to advise on plans for a new government health think-tank, so some of her confidence came back as she realised she probably had until the following week before she'd see him. By which time she just might be able to cope with seeing him again without actually having a nervous breakdown, she prayed.

However, all of that calculating and considering left her woefully unprepared for Friday night after clinic when he barged into her office. 'What the hell is this?' he demanded.

Annabel's legs went weak. She sat down and looked blankly at the sheets of paper he was brandishing. 'Well, if you kept them still for five seconds so I could see—' she began, but then she caught sight of the heading on the top sheet of the fax and paled. 'Where did you get that?' she demanded.

'Where I got it isn't important—'

'That is a confidential fax,' she cried.

'What are you doing, faxing your résumé to the Harefield?'

'I was simply making an enquiry,' she countered. 'Luke, you have no right to have that. This is outrageous. *Outrageous!* That was a highly confidential enquiry. I spoke personally to the medical staffing officer and she assured me no one here would be told anything. Who leaked that to you?'

'Where else have you made enquiries?'

'None of your business.'

He kicked her door shut and she jumped. 'Where?'

'I don't have to answer that.' She swung out of her chair and backed nervously when he advanced, his expression dangerous. 'Don't be silly,' she said huskily. 'You can't beat it out of me.'

'The thought remains tempting,' he growled. He slammed the papers down on her desk. 'What the hell are you playing at, Annie?'

'I thought you were away.'

'I'm back,' he retorted unnecessarily. 'Well?'

Annabel swallowed. 'Isn't it obvious? I'm looking about for another job. Where did you get that copy of my fax—?'

'You left a copy on the machine,' he said tightly. 'My secretary thought I should see it. Why, Annabel? Why did you send this?'

'You know why.'

'Suppose you tell me.'

'I don't want to work with you,' she wailed, angry that he was forcing her to say the words even though they both knew them already.

'Because of Saturday?'

'I'd mostly decided before that. What…happened on Saturday night just makes me more determined. I can't work with you, Luke. I can't stay here. I can't keep telling myself that the past doesn't matter because it does. I'll go mad if I have to keep seeing you.' She reached across to the printer attached to her computer. 'I've written my resignation.' She pulled the top sheet from the tray. 'I was going to give it to your secretary tomorrow but you may as well have it now.'

'Consider it rejected.' Unceremoniously he tore the sheet into shreds and let them fall to the floor. 'You're not going anywhere.'

'You can't do that.' Her mouth open, Annabel gazed down at the remains of her letter. 'It's on the computer. All I have to do is print it again.'

'They'll all be rejected.'

'I was only giving a copy to you out of professional courtesy,' she told him stiffly. 'You have no authority over me. I'm employed by the trust.'

'What do you want from me, Annie?' He looked furious. 'Haven't you had enough blood already? Or is it my resignation you're after this time?'

'Of course not.' She folded her arms tightly around herself, bemused by his questions. As if she could ever provoke such a thing. 'All I want is another job where I don't have to see you all the time. Why can't you just leave me alone?'

'Because I can't,' he ground out. 'Are you blind? How can you not see that? You've got me on the end of a string, like a puppet. I want to stay away from you but I can't. Do you know why that is, Annie?'

At the numbed shake of her head he smiled. 'It's because you alone have always been able to drive every sane, rational thought out of my head. It's because, despite all these

years, nothing's changed. I was going to give you some
space and some time but I can't. I can't because right now
nothing in the world seems more important to me than taking you home and making love to you.' He took a step
forward, his expression determined. 'Only this time it won't
be until you're so ready you're crying out for me and I feel
your body tightening around me in pleasure instead of
pain.'

Annabel felt her face turn scarlet. She backed a step.
'Stay away from me,' she warned huskily.

'But I've just told you I can't,' he said silkily. He took
another step towards her. 'And you weren't fighting me all
the time on Saturday, Annabel. Not at first. I can make you
feel that way again. Come here.'

'Get lost.'

Her office was too small for her to get far enough away
from him to feel safe so instead she tried to skirt past him
to the door. But he caught her before she was even halfway,
one arm curling around her to haul her against him, his
mouth coming down hard on hers. Controlling her with
frustrating ease, he ignored the feeble blows she rained at
his chest, his hands becoming seeking and demanding.

Somehow Annabel managed to twist away. She backed
off quickly from him, one hand still holding her skirt, the
other spread, trembling, in front of her in what suddenly
felt like a frighteningly feeble attempt to fend him off.
'Stop it,' she ordered faintly when he started slowly ad-
vancing towards her again. 'No, Luke.'

'Stop pretending,' he said quietly. 'No more pretending.
Your body's saying yes.' Reaching her, he captured her
arms and spread them apart to reveal the rising shape of
her breasts beneath the jacket he'd unbuttoned and her slip.

Annabel looked down at herself, saw how her puckered
flesh welcomed him and stilled. She wasn't giving in, she

wasn't ever giving in, but somehow, instead of fighting, her hands rose to encircle his wrists where he held her still, holding him instead of pushing him away, her body meekly unresisting as he moved her determinedly towards the wall behind them. 'Luke—'

'Why not?' She tore her stricken gaze away from her own shameless, heaving breasts beneath her slip as he lowered his head to the side of her throat. 'Why not?' he murmured. 'I'll be gentle this time. I was too frantic before. I rushed you. I won't hurt you this time.'

'I'll still leave,' she protested weakly, but he didn't react, didn't blink, didn't even hesitate as he captured her mouth. Suddenly, instead of pushing him away, her hands clung to his wrists as he pressed her back against the cool wall behind her. 'Are you so desperate to hold onto your staff you think you have to seduce them to keep them, Luke?'

'Desperate to hold onto you,' he insisted hoarsely. 'Only you. Don't leave, Annie. Stay. Stay with me here. Give me another chance. I've don't want to lose you again. We can make this work.'

'But I won't be able to bear it,' she whispered. 'I'll sleep with you if that's really what you want but you'll be destroying me.'

'I won't. Hurting you is worse than anything else in the world.'

Annabel turned her head away from him, closing her eyes as his mouth slid hotly across her skin to feel the fast pulse at the side of her throat. 'You'll do it anyway. You might not mean to but you will.'

'I love you. The last thing in the world I want to do is cause you pain.'

Her heart trembled but she was too frightened of his power over her to be anything but cautious. 'You've said you loved me before,' she reminded him tremulously. 'Why should I believe you this time?'

He dropped his arms and stood away from her, his expression oddly defeated. 'What do I have to do to prove it to you? Is it still my career, Annie? Do you still feel you're in competition with it? I thought we'd worked through that but it seems not. What will it take for you to forgive me for the mistakes we made in the past? Do you want me to take some quiet, undemanding job in a backwater for you? Are you asking me to quit as director here so you can stay on in peace?'

She looked up abruptly, meeting his hard green regard with cold shock. 'Would you do that for me?'

'Are you asking me to?'

'If I did, would you?'

His mouth tightened. 'I'm not going to play hypothetical games with you, Annie. Either ask me or don't. Don't fool around.'

She lowered her head and turned away from him, folding her arms protectively as she stared out of her window down onto the hospital lawn below them. 'It's not your job,' she told him unsteadily. 'I understand better about that now. I don't want you to leave here.'

'What, then?'

'I don't understand what you want from me.'

'Everything.' She heard him move behind her, felt him behind her, although he didn't touch her. 'I want everything. You, a home, children, marriage, if you'll have me again.'

Annabel closed her eyes. 'Daddy would be over the moon to hear you say that,' she whispered. 'He's just about given up hope of ever seeing any grandchildren.'

'What about you?'

'I love you.' She'd started to shake again. 'I've loved

you for nine years, including all that time you went away. That's a big chunk of my life, Luke. I'll always love you.'

'Then give me your trust,' he demanded softly. 'Annie, I made mistakes. I left you because I thought that was the right thing to do for both of us. I wanted the chance to achieve something in Boston and I wanted you to have your chance to reach the sort of height in your career that I aspired to in mine.

'I was wrong. I didn't see then that you were the most important thing in my life and I wasn't wise enough to understand that you could be happy meeting less than your full potential with your own career. I need you, Annie. My life has been incomplete without you, I just didn't realise it until I had the chance to fall in love with you all over again. I fought it at first but the night I sent you out with Geoffrey Clancy I almost went mad, waiting for you to come home. Forgive me. Take me back. Give me another chance to make you happy.'

She had no choice. She loved him too much not to trust him, but she also believed him now. 'Yes.' She turned around and flung herself at him. 'Yes,' she sobbed against him as his mouth came down onto hers. 'Yes.'

Some time late the following morning Annabel woke wrapped in Luke's warm arms in her bed. They'd been in too much of a hurry to draw the curtains the previous night and the room was full of summery light. She wiggled around and looked at him. He was beautiful and she ached with love for him. 'I thought I was dreaming,' she said softly when he opened his eyes and smiled at her.

He bent his head and bit gently at her ear. 'Was it a good dream?'

'Mmm.' She arched against him, smiling when one broad

hand slid up from her waist to cup her bare breast posses-
sively. 'Incredibly good. Thank you.'

'For waking you up?'

'For making everything wonderful,' she countered. 'For
loving me again. For being so gentle.'

'But I still hurt you.'

'Only a little bit the first time, but not afterwards.'
Annabel swivelled around to lie atop him, taking command
now. 'I'm a bit stiff but that just means I need practice,'
she told him confidently. He was already aroused and she
came up onto her knees and gently straddled him.

Luke groaned as she took him into her. He curled his
hand around the back of her neck and pulled her down to
him, his mouth covering hers with a passion and urgency
that set her blood racing again. 'I don't mean to rush you
but I have to be at Heathrow to meet Mom in two hours,'
he said hoarsely. 'Come with me and surprise her?'

Annabel stilled, abruptly shocked because until that moment she'd forgotten about Rosemary coming. She sank
down against his thighs, her desire momentarily fading, although the soft sound of protest Luke made at her stillness
suggested his hadn't done the same. 'What will she say
about me?' she asked quietly.

'Probably something like, "About time, idiot boy,"'
Luke told her impatiently. 'Like your father, Mom gave up
hope of grandchildren a long time ago. Around the same
time I told her if she tried setting just one more of her
friends' daughters onto me, I'd probably strangle her.'

Annabel's eyes narrowed. 'Were any of them beautiful?'
she asked huskily.

'You think I cared?' Luke's hands fondled her breasts.
'It's a long, long time since I've had eyes for any women
but belligerent redheads with big grey eyes. You're a pretty
rare breed, Annabel Geddes.'

'Annabel *Stuart*,' Annabel reminded him breathlessly.

'Ah.' He tugged her down and kissed her again. 'Not for long, I'm afraid. In case you didn't notice, we didn't use protection just now. My mother would be horrified if the mother of her first grandchild was merely cohabiting with her son. And she hates flying. She has to see a therapist for weeks before she can get on a plane. To keep her sweet there's going to have to be wedding this week while she's already in town.'

'Just to keep your mother happy,' Annabel agreed, kissing him back. 'Of course, we'll have to invite Daddy and Harry and his wife and Geoffrey and Miriam Frost and then there's the rest of the staff. Next week's too soon to invite Daisy, even though she's been secretly playing matchmaker, because she won't be able to leave hospital for another few weeks, but we could ask Harry to video—'

'Annie?' Luke's hands tightened at her hips and he rocked her forward urgently onto him, his eyes on her breasts, his expression preoccupied. 'My darling, much as I love your sexy little voice, can we talk about the guest list a little later, please?'

'Of course.' Annabel braced her hands on either side of his chest, bent her head and softly kissed him. 'Whatever you say. Even if I didn't love you with all my heart, how could I possibly argue?' She thrust forward gently, her eyes closing blissfully as he slid within her. 'You know you're the boss.'

MILLS & BOON®

Makes any time special™

Mills & Boon publish 29 new titles every month. Select from...

Modern Romance™   Tender Romance™

Sensual Romance™

Medical Romance™   Historical Romance™

4 FREE

books and a surprise gift!

We would like to take this opportunity to thank you for reading this Mills & Boon® book by offering you the chance to take FOUR more specially selected titles from the Medical Romance™ series absolutely FREE! We're also making this offer to introduce you to the benefits of the Reader Service™—

- ★ FREE home delivery
- ★ FREE gifts and competitions
- ★ FREE monthly Newsletter
- ★ Exclusive Reader Service discounts
- ★ Books available before they're in the shops

Accepting these FREE books and gift places you under no obligation to buy, you may cancel at any time, even after receiving your free shipment. Simply complete your details below and return the entire page to the address below. *You don't even need a stamp!*

YES! Please send me 4 free Medical Romance books and a surprise gift. I understand that unless you hear from me, I will receive 6 superb new titles every month for just £2.40 each, postage and packing free. I am under no obligation to purchase any books and may cancel my subscription at any time. The free books and gift will be mine to keep in any case.

M0ZEA

Ms/Mrs/Miss/Mr ....Initials.....................................
BLOCK CAPITALS PLEASE

Surname ....

Address ....

....

....Postcode.................................

Send this whole page to:
UK: FREEPOST CN81, Croydon, CR9 3WZ
EIRE: PO Box 4546, Kilcock, County Kildare (stamp required)